COUNTING BACKWARDS

COUNTING BACKWARDS

LAURA LASCARSO

Atheneum Books for Young Readers
NEW YORK LONDON TORONTO SYDNEY NEW DELHI

ATHENEUM BOOKS FOR YOUNG READERS
An imprint of Simon & Schuster Children's Publishing Division
1230 Avenue of the Americas, New York, New York 10020

ATHENEUM BOOKS FOR YOUNG READERS
is a registered trademark of Simon & Schuster, Inc.
Atheneum logo is a trademark of Simon & Schuster, Inc.
For information about special discounts for bulk purchases,
please contact Simon & Schuster Special Sales at
1-866-506-1949 or business@simonandschuster.com.
The Simon & Schuster Speakers Bureau can bring authors to your live event.
For more information or to book an event, contact the
Simon & Schuster Speakers Bureau at 1-866-248-3049
or visit our website at www.simonspeakers.com.
Also available in an Atheneum Books for Young Readers hardcover edition.
The text for this book is set in ITC New Baskerville.
Manufactured in the United States of America
First Atheneum Books for Young Readers paperback edition August 2013
2 4 6 8 10 9 7 5 3 1
The Library of Congress has cataloged the hardcover edition as follows:
Lascarso, Laura.
Counting backwards / Laura Lascarso. — 1st ed.
p. cm.
Summary: After stealing a car and assaulting a police officer, sixteen-year-old
Taylor is sent to a boarding school that functions as a juvenile psychiatric
correctional facility, where she struggles to hold onto her sanity as she battles her
parents, overbearing therapists, and a group of particularly nasty fellow patients.
ISBN 978-1-4424-0690-2 (hardcover)
[1. Boarding schools—Fiction. 2. Schools—Fiction.
3. Self-control—Fiction. 4. Family problems—Fiction.] I. Title.
PZ7.L3266Co 2012
[Fic]—dc23
2011034783
ISBN 978-1-4424-0691-9 (pbk)
ISBN 978-1-4424-0692-6 (eBook)

For my mother,
my first best friend.

CHAPTER 1

Three weeks ago I tried to run away from home. Now all I want is to go back.

With my thumbnail I etch my name—TAYLOR—on the blue vinyl seat in front of me, over and over in the exact same spot, because the impression lasts only as long as it takes to get from *T* to *R*. I try to keep my mind blank, but I keep thinking about the last time I saw my mom. It was two days ago in the courtroom, where she sat, silent as a turtle, while my father asked the judge's permission for me to carry out my probation in a "maximum-security facility" where I could receive "intense psychiatric care." And the judge, who doesn't know me at all, agreed.

I pull the Sunny Meadows brochure from my pocket and smooth out the creases left over from when my dad first gave it to me and I crushed it into a ball. According to the brochure, Sunny Meadows is a "therapeutic boarding school" in the business of "creating bright futures for exceptional youth," but there's nothing exceptional about what it takes to get into this place—anger, depression, substance abuse, eating disorders, ADHD, OCD . . . The list goes on and on, but none of that is me. I'm normal. I'm *fine*.

The transport van exits off the interstate in Valdosta, and I stick my nose to the cracked window to get some fresh air because I suddenly feel nauseous. It's October now, but the weather is still hot and muggy. I study the landscape of gently rolling pastures as we wind down country roads. I catalog landmarks and signs—New Light Baptist Church, Shady Pines Mobile Home Park, a flaking billboard that says JESUS LOVES YOU. There's no map on the brochure and no address either, "for privacy reasons," but I need to know where they're taking me, just in case I have to find my own way out.

The van pulls into a long, paved driveway, and my chest tightens as my eyes meet with a massive wrought-iron gate.

A gate. A guard. And a chain-link fence that surrounds the campus on all sides. That photo was *not* in the brochure. The fence seems even higher than the one at juvie. As the gate opens, my heart flutters and I massage the knot in my chest, trying to loosen it up, trying to breathe.

The driveway snakes through a huge lawn and dead-ends at a three-story brick building. Spanish moss clings to the branches of the live oak trees and beckons like little ghost hands. The dormitory and its surrounding buildings could pass for any number of private, Southern boarding schools. If it weren't for all the fences.

An escort walks me from the van to the lobby, where I see my dad standing on the other side of the metal detectors. My mom's not with him, and I remind myself I don't care because I'm mad at her anyway. Our eyes meet, and for a moment I have this impulse to run to him so he can hold me tight and tell me everything is going to be all right.

But nothing is right anymore.

Once I'm through the metal detectors, another woman calls me by name, and it sounds cold and robotic on her lips. She motions me into a smaller room, where I recognize my two duffel bags sitting on top of a long, stainless-steel table. They're both unzipped, and a man wearing latex gloves is rifling through my stuff like it's his and not mine.

"Have a seat, Ms. Truwell," the woman says, and presents me with a chair. "Take out your braid. I need to check your head for lice."

I sit down and unravel my braid, letting my long black hair fall past my shoulders in waves. The woman picks through it with pointy cylindrical sticks while I watch the man through the gaps in my hair.

"No electronics," he says, pulling out my MP3 player and dropping it into a bin. Hearing it chink against the hard plastic hurts my ears. I have some of my own recordings on there of my friends playing music, songs that would be hard to replace.

"No sharps," he says, and drops an unopened pack of disposable razors into the bin as well.

"How will I shave my legs?" I ask the woman.

"With supervision."

Supervision? What kind of place is this?

"Nit-free," the woman says. "Have a seat in the lobby. Someone will be down in a minute to show you to your room."

I go out to the lobby, where my father's already occupying one-half of the couch. I sit down on the opposite end, as far away as possible. I'm still not sure why he came. I thought we said our good-byes at juvie when he gave me the Sunny Meadows brochure and I threw it in the trash can. I waited until he left to pick it back out.

"Do you have anything you'd like to say to me?" he asks.

I shake my head. The best way to avoid an argument with my father is to not speak to him at all.

"Taylor," he says again, softer this time, and I risk a glance over at him. He sits with his legs crossed in a trim gray suit with his long black hair pulled into a neat ponytail. Tiny wrinkles line his skin like riverbeds on a map, and there's a tired look in his eyes that's probably my fault too. When I was little, my grandmother used to tell me I looked just like my father, but on the inside we couldn't be more different.

"I want to tell you something," my father says, and I train my eyes straight ahead on the television screen. My father always wants to tell me something, but he never wants to listen. "It's about the Deer."

Deer with a capital *D*. It's my father's clan. Our tribe is Seminole, the Unconquered People. He used to talk about the Seminole Wars fought between our ancestors and the U.S. government down in the River of Grass. When Andrew Jackson's soldiers tried to hunt us down, rape our women, burn our camps, steal our cattle, and put us in cages, we prevailed. My father used to say, *When we could not fight, we ran. When we could not run, we hid. But we never surrendered.*

But he's changed since then. Now he's the one doing the caging.

"The Deer are beautiful creatures," he says, "with lovely doe eyes and a light step. But they are easily frightened—a snapped twig, the chirp of a cricket, the wind in the trees. They do not stop to find where their fear comes from. They flee without thinking, always running, always hunted, never knowing why."

"I am not Deer," I say, because it's the truth. Clan is passed down through your mother, and my own mother is nonnative.

"But you are part of me," he says quietly, forcefully. "As you are part of your grandmother."

I stare at my father's coppery brown eyes, the same shade as my own. He's bringing up my grandmother to remind me of who I am. Or who I was.

"That's why I stole the car?" I say with obvious sarcasm, because he hates it when I disrespect my heritage. "Because I am like the Deer?"

"I don't know why you did it. You won't tell me."

It doesn't matter anymore why I stole that car and tried to run away from my mother's house. Even if I could explain it, my father wouldn't understand. He'd tell me I should have come to him. But our relationship is just one fight after another. And I never wanted to leave my mother, I just wanted her to stay sober.

"I have tried to help you in this manner," he says, "but I'm invisible to you. My words mean nothing. And now you have broken the law. Your criminal record will follow you the rest of your life, yet you never stopped to ask yourself: Why?" He shakes his head. "I've done all I can. That responsibility falls on someone else now."

He sits back, and my resentment gathers like thunderclouds. I study my hands, my fingers, long like my grandmother's, but not nearly as nimble. How can he punish me for trying to leave when he's the one who left us first?

I sense someone standing over us and glance up to see a college-age girl. "Hello, Mr. Truwell." She nods at him and turns to me. "Hi, Taylor, I'm Kayla, your intern-in-residence." She smiles brightly at me and I know I should smile back, but I don't feel like pretending. I want to go home.

"What's an intern-in-residence?" I ask her, trying not to sound too suspicious.

"It's kind of like a big sister. Basically, I'm here to help you with your transition into Sunny Meadows and answer any questions you might have. I'll be leading our group discussions, and I have an apartment down the hall from you, so I'll always be available if you need something. Why don't we all go upstairs and check out your room?"

I don't want to check out my room or go any farther than the lobby. I want to make a mad dash for the fence and climb, but I force my feet to follow Kayla and my father into the stairwell and up three flights of stairs. We enter a long, fluorescent-lit hallway that makes my skin look sickly and green. The doors to the rooms are wide open, but the floor is deserted. Kayla tells us the girls are in group activities on the second floor and they'll be back soon.

"Why are all the doors open?" I ask.

"We always keep them open. At Sunny Meadows, privacy is a privilege."

My stomach turns. Privacy a privilege? Even with my mom, I've always kept my door shut. That was my right, not a privilege.

"Sunny Meadows is based on a merit system," Kayla says, "where residents earn privileges through cooperation and care."

"Like privacy?"

"Yes, also music and TV, Internet and telephone time, makeup and nail polish, soda and vending-machine snacks, all those little extras."

I think of my confiscated MP3 player. I can live without all the other stuff, but no music?

"What do I have to do to get privileges?"

"Just show us you're a ready and willing participant in the program."

She must be talking about my "rehabilitative program." I read about it in the Sunny Meadows brochure. I've got the next six months to complete it. And my dad told me if I try to run away, it'll be a breach of my probation and I'll be hauled back to juvie.

But only if they find me.

Kayla stops in front of an open door and motions for me to go ahead of her, but my shoes are glued to the floor. I can't go any farther. My father takes hold of my arm and guides me into the room.

The cinder-block walls are a custard color with one tiny window high up in the corner. It's fixed with some sort of shatterproof glass that makes the outside look foggy. My duffel bags are already here, sitting beside the twin bed. There's a desk, a chair, and a dresser with a mirror bolted to the wall. The polished metal is like the kind of mirror in playground bathrooms—dim and creepy. The room smells like hand sanitizer, and it's cold enough to make me shiver. Goose bumps form all along my arms, and I bite down hard on my lip to keep from crying.

"I'll let you say your good-byes," Kayla says, and backs out of the room.

I turn to my father, because he must realize by now what a mistake this is. I don't belong in a place like Sunny Meadows. I'm not crazy.

"Dad, don't leave me here."

He says nothing, only strokes his chin and surveys the room.

"I won't do anything like that again, I swear."

"Taylor, it is too late. You brought this on yourself."

"I could do my probation at your house if you want. I don't have to live with Mom."

"Give it time, Taylor. Give this program a try."

"Dad, I don't belong here."

"This experience will be good for you. It will be a positive change."

He's not listening to me or he doesn't care. He's going to dump me in here and forget about me for the next six months, and by the time I get out, I might not even recognize myself. I'll be no better off than when I got here, because my mother will still be a drunk and my father will still be cold and unforgiving. And I'll still be . . . me.

"This is just like what you did to Mom," I say, thinking about the times she came out of rehab, how every time she lost a little more of herself. "You're locking me up just like her."

He sighs and looks away. "No, Taylor, I'm doing this so you don't turn into your mother—an impulsive, reckless, selfish woman."

I glare at him. He has no right to say that about her. It's his fault she's the way she is. He's the one who left her, who left *us*.

"Get out," I say. When he doesn't move, I say it again louder. "Get *out*."

"Your anger is bigger than you are. You let it control you."

"You don't know anything about me," I say to him. I am a too-full jar about to spill over.

"You're right, I don't." He stands there like a statue, unmoved. I want him to know what it feels like to be me. I want him to hear me for once in my life.

"I hate you." Three words I've never uttered to anyone before, but I say them to him because if he's going to leave me here in this strange place with its hospital smells and weird rules, then I want him to just *go*.

"I'm sorry you feel that way," he says, every word clipped and measured, like he's talking to a business partner and not his own daughter. "I'll return soon for a visit."

"Don't bother. I won't want to see you."

He nods slowly. "Well, then. I suppose this is good-bye." He nods once more and walks out of the room. I listen to his footsteps retreating down the hallway, the sound of him speaking with someone else, then the stairwell door opening and shutting, followed by a silence that echoes in my mind.

My chest tightens, and it feels like a fist inside my rib cage, squeezing my lungs so I can't draw enough air. My breathing is erratic and shallow, like all the oxygen has been sucked out of the room. I'm nauseous and dizzy and I suddenly have to move. I have to get out of here.

I dash out to the hallway and head for the nearest exit. I knead my breastbone with my knuckles until my chest opens up and I'm able to take a few quick breaths. I punch down on the door's metal bar and throw my weight against the door, but it's stuck.

Not stuck. Locked. I'm trapped. *Trapped.*

Behind me a voice taunts, "You're not getting out that way, girlfriend."

CHAPTER 2

I spin around to see a girl my own age, tall and thin as a pine. Her long blond hair is pulled into a tight ponytail, and she tilts her head and smiles at me like some demented flight attendant.

"That's where they keep the boys," she says. "Behind door number one. But you'll never get through that way. They keep it locked up tight."

"Who are you?" I ask, knuckling my chest as hard as I can. I'll leave a bruise, but at least I can breathe.

"You must be Taylor Truwell." She offers her hand, but I only stare at it. "I'm Margo Blanchard, your new peer mentor."

"My what?"

"Peer mentor. It was my therapist's idea. He thinks I need to take on more responsibilities to prepare for my release, but between you and me, I'm not ready to leave just yet."

"Why not?"

She shrugs. "This place has its charm. But enough about me. Tell me, where are you from?"

"Tampa."

"Are you Cuban?"

"No. Seminole Indian. Half."

"What's the other half?"

"German, English, some Polish. How about you?"

"French, mostly." She steps closer and inspects my face. "Are you wearing makeup?"

I reach up to touch my cheek. "No."

"I have makeup privileges. We should give each other makeovers." She claps her hands excitedly. "I just got this new liquid eyeliner that would really make your eyes pop. And I've perfected my smoky eyes technique. With a little shadow and some sculpting . . ."

She rattles on about makeup and beauty tips, but I only half listen because in the meantime a girl with curly red hair emerges from the room next to mine. I listen as she raps on my door frame in a complicated pattern. It sounds like a coded message, frenzied and desperate.

"There's no one home, Charlotte," Margo says to her. "Come meet Taylor." The girl glances over at me, and I'm about to say hello when she suddenly turns and sprints back to her room.

"That reminds me, Charlotte, I brought you something." Margo heads for Charlotte's room, but as soon as she crosses the threshold, Charlotte starts screaming her head off. Margo steps back, looking slightly annoyed, and the screaming stops. When Margo tries to re-enter, the scream-ing starts up again like some weird human alarm system.

I yank on the stairwell door again, but it still doesn't budge.

"I thought we were past this," Margo says to her as a woman thunders down the hall toward us.

"What's this all about?" the woman calls to Margo, hook-ing her thumbs over her thick black belt, where all sorts of gadgets—a walkie-talkie, a miniature Maglite, and more—hang like charms on a bracelet. She wears a polo shirt with khaki pants, which means she must be Sunny Meadows staff.

"Charlotte and I were just practicing a little scream ther-apy," Margo says, and winks at me like it's an inside joke.

"No more," the woman says to Charlotte, then aims one hot-pink talon at Margo. "You know better than to get her going. What are you doing on this floor, anyway?"

"I'm Taylor's peer mentor," she says, and smiles demonically at me. The woman shakes her head, and Margo giggles. I can't tell if Margo's *trying* to scare me or if she's sincerely insane.

"On my floor, you mind your manners," the woman says to Margo. Then she turns to me. "And you, don't let this one be a bad influence."

I don't know her, I want to say, but the woman's already walking away.

"That's Tracy," Margo says. "As far as floor safeties go, you could do a lot worse."

"Safeties?"

"Haven't you noticed all the beefy men and full-bodied women? Those guys and gals are doing everything they can to keep us safe and secure. But back to the task at hand." She pivots toward Charlotte's room, where Charlotte is now camped out on her bed, scribbling furiously in an open book. Margo reaches into her boot and pulls out a pack of twistable crayons, which capture Charlotte's attention as she fixes her eyes on the package.

"I'm just going to throw them in, okay?" Margo says.

Charlotte nods while one fist clenches the blanket on her bed, as though it's physically hurting her to have someone enter her room. I feel sorry for her. I even know a little how she feels. I don't like people invading my personal space either.

Margo approaches slowly, tosses the pack on the corner of Charlotte's bed, and backs out of her room. "Now, tell Taylor your rule, or else how will she know?"

Charlotte stares at me with a wild look in her eyes. "No one's allowed in my room. *No one.*"

I nod enthusiastically. That won't be a problem.

Margo swipes her hands together as though her job is done, and I hope maybe now she'll leave. But instead of heading for the stairwell door, she goes toward my room. I follow her inside and stand guard next to my two duffel bags.

"Do you smoke?" she asks, retrieving a cigarette and matches from her other boot.

"I'm trying to quit," I say, even though I've never tried smoking. My mother has enough bad habits for the both of us. "Besides, isn't smoking against the rules?"

"Not my rules." She strikes a match and lights her cigarette, taking a long drag. "It's a real inconvenience that they don't let me have matches. Though I'll admit, things did get a little out of control the last time."

"The last time?"

Her answer is a massive cloud of bluish smoke. I hear Tracy's voice in the hallway, "You smell cigarettes?" followed by her heavy footsteps heading our way fast.

"At least when I'm on the outside, I might get to finish an entire cigarette," Margo says, and takes three more quick puffs.

"Put it out," I hiss. I'm about to get totally busted, and it's only my first day here. Margo smiles and throws her lit cigarette into the trash can while I fan the room, trying to disperse the smoke. She tosses me her matches like a hot potato, and I'm about to peg her back when I see one of Tracy's black boots in the doorway. I make a fist around the matchbook and try to act natural.

"Who's smoking in here?" Tracy asks, staring directly at Margo. She knows who's responsible.

"Martha Washington told me to do it," Margo says. "She said if I didn't, she'd dye my hair brown."

Tracy shifts her weight to the other hip; she doesn't seem too impressed.

"Empty those boots, Margo. Don't make me frisk you."

Margo huffs, takes off both boots, and turns them over, dumping everything onto the linoleum floor—cigarettes, an empty book of matches, a box of Tic Tacs, loose change, a few dollar bills, and a tube of lip gloss. Tracy pulls a plastic bag out of a little black container on her belt and holds it open while Margo dumps everything inside.

"Take me away," Margo says, and holds out her wrists like she's waiting to be handcuffed. I've been handcuffed for real and it wasn't much fun. Tracy just shakes her head and waits for Margo to pass in front of her. "See you tomorrow," Margo says to me, "if they let me out."

"That's enough," Tracy says, and nudges her along. "Peer mentor. I'm going to have to talk to somebody about this."

I worry about where Tracy is taking her, maybe to a padded cell. That was pretty dumb of Margo to smoke a cigarette, knowing she'd get caught. But how bad could the punishment be?

I glance across the hall to see a girl in the opposite room, glaring at me with eyes like knives. "FYI, new girl," she says. "You make friends with Margo Blanchard, you make enemies with us."

Us? I glance around her room. She's the only one in there. Maybe she has split personalities or something. I have no more expectations for normal in this place. I can't believe my dad left me here. These people are crazy. If my mother knew what this place was really like . . .

My mother.

I have to call her. My mom knows me better than anyone else. She knows I'm not crazy.

I find Kayla's apartment at the other end of the hallway— the only one with the door closed. I knock, and a moment later she opens it.

"Hi, Taylor, what do you need?"

"I'd like to call my mom."

Kayla frowns. "I'm sorry, but you haven't earned that privilege yet."

"I really miss her," I say as a desperate feeling creeps in. "I just need a few minutes."

"It takes three days of good decision making to earn a phone call."

"Please, Kayla, I really need to talk to her. I never got to say good-bye."

Her eyes search mine, and I say a silent prayer she'll grant me my request. Her face softens, and she looks past me into the empty hallway. "You'll need to make it quick."

Kayla walks me down to the shorter end of the L-shaped

hallway to what she calls the common room, which is just a weathered couch and chairs in front of an ancient television set. She points to the phone, the old-fashioned kind with the curly cord so you can't go too far with it. "Five minutes," she says, "and I'm going to be monitoring your end of the conversation."

I call my mom's cell phone and wait ring after ring. It takes forever for her to finally pick up.

"Hello?" she croaks.

"Mom, it's me."

"Taylor?"

I glance up at the clock hanging on the wall—it's four p.m. on a Sunday. "Are you *just* getting up?"

"No, no, honey, I was taking a nap. Hold on, give me a second here. . . ."

I hear some scraping, the fridge door opening, and the sound of liquid pouring into a glass. Hopefully it's water. I glance back at the clock. Almost a minute gone.

"Baby," she says at last, "how are you?"

"Not good, Mom. I'm at this place—Sunny Meadows—and the people here are . . ." I glance over at Kayla. "Disturbed."

"They are?"

"Yes. Completely. You need to come get me."

"Taylor, you just got there. Why don't you try to make some friends, at least?"

Is she kidding me? I don't want to make friends with these people.

"Mom, please. If you leave right now, we could be back home by tomorrow morning." I wait, but hear only her breath. "Mom?"

"I know this is hard for you, Taylor, but your father thinks it's for the best."

Who cares what he thinks? When has she ever done what he's told her to do?

"How about you, Mom? What do *you* think?"

I hear one long, endless sigh. "I think we should give it a try."

I feel my anger rising. There's nothing wrong with me, and even if there was, my mom's been through rehab enough times to know it's a waste of time and money. A waste of life.

"This isn't *we* giving it a try, Mom, it's *me*. Alone. Trapped in here with the crazies."

"Give it a week, Taylor. And make some friends. Find strength in others."

I suppress a groan. I hate it when she gives me her generic rehab slogans. "I don't want to find strength in others, Mom. I want to come home." I can't make it any plainer. If she really loved me, if she cared about me at all, she'd come up here and bring me home.

But maybe she doesn't want me back. She can do anything

she wants now. She no longer has to keep up the charade of being somebody's mother.

"What about your episodes, Taylor?"

She's talking about the feeling in my chest, the times when I can't catch my breath, which is her fault as far as I'm concerned, hers and my father's. But I could handle it if they'd just leave me alone. I know I could.

"There is *nothing* wrong with me," I tell her.

She's quiet after that, and I feel my whole body go rigid and cold, like a glacier. I'm a mass of impenetrable ice. Nothing can touch me. Not her, not anyone.

"I know you're unhappy," she says at last, "and I want you to come home, but . . . your father's right. This is the right place for you, for now."

"I guess he's right about a lot of things, huh?" She knows what I'm talking about—all those times my dad tried to take custody away from her and I lied for her. For us. I never told him about all the nights she went out drinking or all the times she was late picking me up from school. How I learned to drive when I was thirteen, just in case she showed up somewhere and couldn't drive home.

"Listen, Taylor . . . I just want to say . . . I love you."

I say nothing because I feel nothing. Even if I did, I wouldn't say it, because I know that's what she wants to hear. Kayla clears her throat and points to the clock. I save my mother the trouble of saying good-bye and hang up the phone. My hands are trembling. I shove them deep into my pockets.

"It sounds like your mother wants you to get help," Kayla says.

I ignore her and walk out of the common room, back down the yellow hallway to the room that's supposed to be mine. I drag my red duffel bag to the corner of the room where I can't be seen from the hallway and dig around for the secret pocket I sewed into the inside of the liner. That's where I keep the birthday money and allowance I don't want my mom to "borrow." When my fingers brush against the money—nearly five hundred dollars in all—my chest opens up a little and I take a deep breath. I might be trapped in this place, but I'm not helpless. I'll make a new plan and leave Sunny Meadows just as I came.

Alone.

CHAPTER 3

That night I have a nightmare. I sit up with a jolt to find myself in a stranger's room. Then I realize it's mine—Sunny Meadows. My pulse throbs in my throat; my hair is sweaty and matted to my skin. I kick off the covers and pace the floor to lift the fog of sleep.

"Shut up!" the girl from across the hall shouts. The night safety pokes her head into my doorway.

"Bad dream," I say. She just points me to my bed.

I climb back in and cover my face with Tatters, my blanket from childhood that is just a square of faded material now. My grandmother sewed it for me when I was little, and I've kept it all this time. Its scent of home is swiftly fading, replaced by the institutional nothing smell of Sunny Meadows. I lie there and try to think of a better place, a safe place. I remember my grandmother's porch in the nighttime, where we slept during the summer because it was too hot indoors. I can almost hear the rise and fall of her voice as she spun tales of our people: Panther—God's favored one, and the Terrible Twins, Thunder and Lightning, and my favorite character, Rabbit, who used his cunning and wit to outsmart the bigger animals who were always trying to eat him. I want to conjure up the night sounds on the reservation—the hoot of a barred owl, the buzzing of cicadas, yard dogs baying at the moon—but the only sounds here are the air conditioner cutting off and on and the crinkling of the plastic mattress liner beneath me. Even worse is the sad realization that I've forgotten more than I can remember.

Then I hear faint music . . . a guitar. I sit up in bed and glance around the room, trying to figure out where it's coming from. I slide out of bed and search the room for a speaker or a radio but find none. In the hallway all is quiet, save for the snores of the other girls.

Back in my room I trace the music to its source, the floor. No, an air vent in the floor. I drop down to my knees and put my ear to the vent, where I can hear it better; the music drifts up through the metal duct like a ghostly lullaby.

I hear a man's voice, quick and severe, and the music's gone, leaving behind only the hum of the air conditioner. I kneel there a moment longer. Maybe I imagined it.

I pull my pillow off the bed and drop it next to the vent. I lie back and stare up at the moonlight filtering through the foggy window. In a groggy, half-dream state I watch the square of window turn from black to blue to pink and finally the white dawn of a new day. Shortly after there's a loud, jarring buzzer, and the safety comes by to make sure I'm up and getting ready for breakfast downstairs in thirty minutes.

Monday morning. My first day at another new school. My mom had this pep talk whenever I'd be getting ready for my first day at a new school: *Just think of all the new friends you're going to make, Taylor. All those people who can't wait to meet you. . . .*

It worked when I was young, but by middle school, I got tired of making friends and having to leave them behind every time we moved because we couldn't pay the rent or my mom decided it was time to move on. If you don't get attached in the first place, there's no one to say good-bye to. My freshman year of high school I started hanging out with this group of guys who were already out of school. They were in a band—Choleric Kindness. I was kind of like their kid sister or groupie, showing up at the warehouse where they practiced. They never seemed to mind me being there, and the music and the constant stream of people coming in and out made it so I never had to talk too much about myself.

They're probably wondering what happened to me. I haven't seen them since before I tried to run away.

I open my closet, bypassing the pleated navy skirts and going straight for the pants. The starched fabric is itchy against my skin and smells like industrial laundry detergent. The shirt collar feels too tight around my throat, so I undo the top two buttons—it's a little better. I run a comb through my frazzled hair and try weaving it into a French braid, but it comes out loose and lopsided, so I unravel it and throw it into a regular old braid, then line up along the hallway with the other girls. The safety calls roll, and I learn that Brandi is the name of the girl in the room across from mine. She gives me a dirty look when my name is called.

Down in the dining room there's a continental breakfast waiting. The food looks washed out—the fruit not quite ripe, the breads dry and stiff as cardboard. I grab a bagel and an individually packaged strawberry jelly, then notice the Sunny Meadows guys for the first time. They're in their own dining room, separated from ours by the kitchen, doing the same morning shuffle. I glance around the room for Margo, but don't see her anywhere. She can't *still* be locked up. Meanwhile most of the other girls have all settled into their table groupings. There's an empty table across the room, and I head for it.

A few minutes later Charlotte comes over and sits down across from me. I'm a little nervous that she might start screaming at me, but I tell her good morning anyway. She nods without looking up from what she's doing, which is cutting her toast into tiny bits and then delicately placing them into her mouth one piece at a time. Like the knocking, there's a pattern to it. After two bites, she takes a sip of water, then wipes her mouth with the napkin. And each time she wipes her mouth, she folds the napkin over so that her lips never touch the same spot twice.

I'm so fascinated by her curious behavior that I don't realize Brandi and her friends are at the table next to ours until they start launching bread crusts our way, aiming for Charlotte. A piece gets stuck in her hair, and they practically scream with laughter. I glare at Brandi while Charlotte stares at her toast, trying to ignore them, but her face is red and splotchy and I'm afraid she's going to start crying at any moment. I tear off a piece of my bagel and throw it back at them. It hits Brandi's shirtfront, then drips to the ground, leaving behind a pink jammy smear.

"You little bitch," Brandi snarls. She stands and takes a step toward me. I lay my hands flat on the table. My muscles tense, and I estimate it will take about two seconds for her to reach me. Do I fight her or do I run?

"Clean up this mess," a safety says. She gets between me and them, blocking them from my view. *Never take your eyes off your assailant.* The echoes of Andy—one of my mom's ex-boyfriends, a security guard—plays in my head.

Charlotte sits there tensely, like she's afraid to move, while I pick the crusts off the floor. The other girls shoot me scathing looks as they pass by, and I notice they're all wearing the same large, gold hoop earrings.

"Sorry about that," Charlotte whispers to me in a tiny voice.

"Don't be. They're the jerks, not you." I throw the bundle in the trash, then take my place at the end of the line, where I can keep an eye on the girls. During walkover the safeties lead us in a herd to the school and I see the guys again, coming from the opposite direction, being driven across the lawn like cattle.

The school building is just one story and looks much newer than the dorms, with one carpeted hallway down the center and classrooms on either side. The safeties take up positions against the wall and keep a close watch, calling out whenever someone makes physical contact or gets too loud.

I go to the office to get my pack of ballpoint pens—our approved writing utensils—along with some folders, a backpack, and a class schedule. They put me in all average classes, probably based on my poor performance at the end of tenth grade. My two weeks in juvie probably set me back even more. I used to care about things like perfect attendance and GPA. I used to make really good grades, but not anymore.

I find my way to first period, American history, where there are about twenty or so kids already there. My stomach drops as I see Brandi and her friends among them. This is not how I want to start the day.

The teacher, Mr. Chris, introduces me to the other students while the girls giggle obnoxiously. Brandi seems to be the alpha female. When she stops laughing, the rest quiet down. Of course the only empty seat is the one behind her.

Mr. Chris says we'll be assembling our Revolutionary War mobiles and then goes through this long talk about "sharps," how they're learning tools and it's important that we respect them as such, that if anyone misuses "sharps," they'll be escorted to the front office, and he'll be counting "sharps" at the end of class. If there are any missing, there will be "serious consequences." I remember my razors and wonder if that's what sharps are, so I lean across the aisle and ask the guy next to me.

"Scissors," he says with a smile, and draws one finger across his neck, like he's slicing his own throat. I face forward, thinking the next time I have a question, I'll ask the teacher.

The male safety comes around with a box of scissors—sharps. They're the old-fashioned metal kind with rounded tips and dull blades. Still, with enough force they could definitely break skin. I glance around the room and wonder if they're worried about us cutting ourselves or one another. Maybe both.

I get my worksheet and cut out these strips of paper with facts on them, which are supposed to be ordered on construction paper like a time line. I'm arranging my facts and pasting—with actual paste—and it's not bad, a little Zen even, when the same kid from before strikes up a conversation.

"You Mexicana?" he asks with a Spanish accent I didn't hear before.

"No."

"Puerto Rican?"

"No." This could go on all day. "I'm American Indian—Seminole."

"You got a boyfriend?"

I glance over, and he licks his lips suggestively.

"You don't want to mess with her, Sulli," Brandi says. "You don't know where she's been."

"Jealous, baby?" Sulli says to her with a slimy smile. Brandi shoots him a death stare.

"Trust me, Trailer. You're *not* his type." With a flip of her ratty hair, Brandi turns back around. I glare at the back of her head and wish I could think of something biting and clever to say, but my comebacks always come too late.

Mr. Chris calls for us to clean up, and the safety comes around to collect the scissors. I drop mine into the box. At the front of the class Mr. Chris counts them—out loud. Why out loud? Maybe to build suspense.

"We have one sharp missing," he announces, shaking his head sorrowfully, like someone has died. Everyone glances around the room. Brandi smiles wickedly at me.

"Let's assume this was an accident," Mr. Chris says. "I'm going to turn my back. If the missing sharp doesn't appear after one minute, we'll be forced to search your properties."

He might be crazier than the class because he actually *turns his back* on the psychos and the minute goes by, terrifyingly slow. No one comes forward, so the safety lines us up along the back of the room where there's a ton of books in stacks— mostly biographies. I scan the titles while the safety goes through our backpacks. He gets to my stuff, and I remember the book of matches I stuffed in there to give back to Margo.

Crap.

"Here," the safety says. He pulls a pair of scissors out of my backpack and holds them up high like a cereal-box prize. "Hidden in her folder."

"I didn't put those there," I tell Mr. Chris. Meanwhile Brandi and her friends can hardly contain themselves. Could it be any more obvious?

"Everyone else may go," Mr. Chris says with his eyes trained on me.

Sulli winks as he passes by, and Brandi swipes a pair of scissors right out of the box on Mr. Chris's desk. Nobody sees it but me. Is this selective sight or what? I should tell on her, but she's already out the door.

"I swear I didn't take them," I say to Mr. Chris. "Someone put them there to make me look bad."

"I believe you," he says, like he'd believe me whether it was true or not. "But it's very important you leave the sharps here, with me. I wouldn't want you to hurt yourself accidentally. You don't want to hurt yourself, do you, Taylor?"

"No, I don't."

"And you don't want to hurt anyone else, do you?"

"No," I say, even though there is someone I wouldn't mind hurting a little.

"So, let's start over," he says, smiling inanely at me. "And tomorrow you can tear out the rest of your project. It won't be as neat, but it will be safe."

He calls on the safety to escort me to my next class, and I know that I'm outnumbered and outmatched. I need help from someone who knows the score.

Someone like Margo Blanchard.

By the time lunch rolls around, I have the beginnings of a headache, and the noise in the cafeteria makes it worse. I collect my cardboard tray, which has been prepackaged according to my "dietary needs." Apparently my needs consist of ambiguous meats and overcooked vegetables.

I scan the lunchroom for Margo, but she's still MIA. Charlotte is sitting at a table by herself, so I make my way over. Halfway there something hits my ankle and I lurch forward. I fight to catch my balance, but it's already too late. My tray falls to the floor at the same time my knees hit the ground.

My kneecaps hurt like crazy and my left hand is crunched painfully beneath my wrist, but luckily, there's no gravy on my face. Then I hear them above me, howling like a pack of wolves.

"Smooth move, Trailer." I glance up at Brandi and realize she tripped me. I've been the new kid enough times to know that if I don't stand up for myself now, it'll only continue. I jump to my feet and lunge for her, but someone gets between us—a guy—and I push him instead. But he's big and solid, so I end up falling back. I glare up at him—where did he even come from?—while the cafeteria falls silent.

"What the hell?" I shout at him. When he doesn't respond, I storm away, leaving my tray behind on the floor. Maybe he's another one of Brandi's psycho boyfriends. Who knows and who cares?

I head for the exit door. Thankfully, it's not locked. Fresh air and sunlight envelop me, and I take a couple of quick steps, about to run. Then my eyes adjust to the light, and I find myself in a concrete courtyard that's closed off on two sides by the building and the other two sides by *another* chain-link fence. A fence within a fence. In-credible.

"Welcome to the pen." I glance to my left and see Margo. Other than the safety manning the door, she's the only person out here. The midday sun lights up her lush blond hair so it looks like a halo of white fire surrounding her pale face.

"Do you know what the worst feeling in the world is?" she asks.

I know the worst feeling in the world. It's the fist in my chest that won't let me breathe.

She holds up two cigarettes. "Having a cigarette in your hand and no way to light it."

She must be asking after her matches. I'm eager to be rid of them, but I don't want her to get in trouble again—I need some peer mentoring. "What about him?" I ask, nodding at the safety.

She waves her hand dismissively. "I'll be discreet."

I don't believe her, but I unhook my backpack from my shoulders, reach in, and toss the book over to her. She catches it in one hand, then holds a cigarette out to me. "You want one?"

"No thanks."

She shrugs and turns away from the safety and the surveillance camera mounted to the building, then lights both cigarettes. "Hang on to these for me," she says, handing me the matches. "Keep me out of trouble."

I glance back toward the safety—he seems to be purposely *not* looking—and sidle up next to her. She looks like a walrus with both cigarettes dangling from her lips. "That can't be good for you," I say.

"Nothing in moderation."

"So, where have you been?" I ask. "Since yesterday?"

"I spent the evening in a time-out room, which is the closest thing we have to a spa around here."

I think back to the handbook Kayla gave me last night. Time-out rooms. "For when residents need a safe place to reflect on their choices." I shudder involuntarily. It doesn't sound like a spa to me.

"They put you in there just for smoking?"

"Ever since the incident on the second floor, the dorm safeties have gotten a lot stricter with me about matches—a real bummer when you love smoking as I do."

"What was the incident?"

"A *tiny* trash fire," she says. "Not even my fault. Not really."

"What's it like in there?" I ask. "In the time-out rooms?"

"A stiff cocktail of mind-numbing boredom, sensory deprivation, and isolation."

"Sounds bad."

She nods. "But effective."

She makes an O with her mouth and pushes out smoke rings . . . one, two, three. I watch them float in the air for a few seconds, then drift apart. I hook my fingers around the warm metal of the chain-link fence and stare past the lawn at the wrought-iron gate attached to the even larger chain-link fence. Beyond that, freedom.

"So, Taylor, what brings you to Sunny Meadows?"

Something I'd rather not talk about, I think. "I got into some trouble at home."

"*Obviously.*" We're quiet for a moment. Then she asks, "So, what'd you do?"

I shrug without answering.

"It's my job to know these things," she says. "I *am* your peer mentor."

"I stole a car," I say, hoping that will be enough.

"What kind of car was it?"

"Not a very nice one."

"First-time offender?"

"More or less."

Technically I stole two cars before the last one. The first time I chickened out and came back, returned the keys to where my mom's barfly friend had left them on the kitchen counter. The second time didn't really count because it was my mom's car. She went out drinking one night and there was no food in our apartment, so I drove over to the warehouse where Choleric Kindness was practicing. Trey—he's their drummer—asked me to come back with him to his apartment, and I had nothing better to do, so I went. At his place, he tried to hook up with me, but I told him I had a boyfriend. I think he knew I was lying, but he backed off and we spent the rest of the night watching TV and eating Totino's pizzas. I didn't want to go home that night. I knew what would be waiting for me—my mom, drunk, or with a guy, maybe both, or else still at the bar—so when Trey offered to let me stay the night on his couch, I said yes.

But my dad tracked me down the next morning, totally furious. It was such a scene, with Trey doing everything he could to convince my father that *nothing* happened, which I told my dad again later, but did he believe me?

"Did you get arrested?" Margo asks, bringing me back to the conversation.

"Yeah. At a gas station."

"Were you robbing it?"

"No, I was getting some gas. I guess I stole that, too."

"Where were you going?"

"I don't know," I say, and it's the truth. I had no idea where I was going. I just had to get away.

"Sounds like a half-assed plan to me."

I chuckle at that because she's absolutely right. "Yeah, I guess it was."

The double doors to the cafeteria open, and more kids and safeties begin to file out. Margo drops her lit cigarettes on the ground and crushes them with her shoe, then tosses them into the trash can. I glance inside it to make sure they're not still burning. When I look up, Brandi and three of her friends are making their way across the pen. My hands ball up into fists as Brandi smiles and waves at me. Margo blows her a kiss.

"Are you friends with them?" I ask.

Margo laughs. "Who? The Latina Queens? Not quite."

"Latina Queens? They don't look Hispanic."

"The girl who started it was—is. She got released over the summer, but the tradition lives on. The rest of them are sweet Georgia peaches. Aren't they darling with their trashy little accessories?"

She can only mean their gold hoop earrings. And no, they're not darling in any way. I watch as they thread themselves through a group of guys who appear too old to be in high school—Sulli among them. The guys wear their shirts with the top few buttons undone and their sleeves rolled up, showing off their tattoos. Their style complements the Latina Queens' hiked-up skirts and too-small shirts. I've never been to a boarding school before—therapeutic or not—but it amazes me how subjective the dress code is, even with uniforms.

"They're probably going to jump you," Margo says while inspecting her fingernails.

"What? Why?"

"Because that's what they do."

I'm a little surprised by her honesty. And her lack of concern for my well-being. Is this what a peer mentor is supposed to do?

"Thanks for the heads-up," I say sarcastically.

"No problem. I'm sure you could convince them to jump me instead."

I remember yesterday when Brandi warned me not to make friends with Margo. "Why is that?" I ask her.

She sighs. "A while back they wanted me to join their silly gang, but I declined—politely, of course. They've hated me ever since. It's seriously killing my popularity. Girls only talk to me when they're not around."

I remember how frightened Charlotte seemed this morning when they were picking on her. Stupid bullies. I decide then that I'm on Margo's side, which is against the Latina Queens. "I guess I shouldn't be talking to you then," I say to her.

"No, you shouldn't. But doesn't it feel forbidden and a little bit dangerous?"

I smile and glance up to see a tall, lanky guy approaching. He flashes Margo a lazy half smile as his longish hair falls over one eye like a carefully executed accident. Then I see someone else following him over, the guy from the lunchroom, the one who got in the middle of my spat with Brandi.

"*Mon ange*," the pretty boy says to Margo while I check out his friend. He's got military short hair, gray eyes, and long, curling lashes. His nose is slightly crooked, like maybe it's been broken, and there's a scar on his upper lip in the shape of a sickle moon. Maybe he's some kind of junior safety, like the ROTC at my last high school.

"Hey, babe," Margo says with a smile. "Taylor Truwell, this is Victor DeMatais and A.J. Guttering. Guys, Taylor."

"*Enchanté, ma chèrie,*" Victor says to me. Margo reminds him that he's not taking orders right now, so could he please speak *English*?

"I apologize. A pleasure to meet you, Taylor. Any friend of Margo's is a friend of mine."

"Thanks," I say, and glance over at his friend, but he says nothing.

"There's a soccer game this afternoon," Victor says. "You girls coming?"

"I don't know, Vic," Margo says. "I really need to wash my hair."

Victor plucks up a lock of her golden hair, twines it in his fingers, and kisses it, all without drawing any attention from the safeties. "I always play better with you there," he croons, and slips something into her palm. A.J. shifts to block them from the safety's line of sight. I notice a thin silver chain around A.J.'s neck that disappears underneath his uniform. He catches me staring and adjusts his collar so that it's hidden completely.

"Until next time, Taylor," Victor says, tipping an imaginary hat in my direction. "See you two lovely ladies later."

A.J. says nothing, only holds my gaze a moment longer and walks off with Victor.

"That's our connection," Margo says after they've left. "If you ever need anything, Victor and A.J. will get it for you."

Anything?

"Is Victor your boyfriend?"

"'Relationships between the sexes are to remain platonic,'" Margo says, reciting from the Sunny Meadows handbook.

"What'd he give you?"

She opens her hand to reveal . . . a box of orange Tic Tacs?

"That's it? I was expecting a hand grenade or a pocket knife, at least."

She smiles. "They're my favorite. The perfect combination of citrus and sunshine and only one and a half calories each."

I look after the pair of them, talking with some guys on the other side of the pen. "What's up with Victor's friend?"

"Who? A.J.?"

"Yeah. He got between me and Brandi in the lunchroom. Right before I came out here, she tripped me and I went to push her, but he got in the way."

"Did he say anything to you?"

"No—just . . . looked at me."

"How very curious." She taps her chin with one slender finger. "Maybe he likes you."

"What? He doesn't even know me."

"Why else would he keep you from getting in trouble?"

"He wasn't. He was just—protecting Brandi."

"A.J. hates Brandi."

"He does?"

"Yeah, we all do."

It must have been an accident, then. But he sure did get there fast, and when he looked at me, it was like he was telling me to back off. Maybe it was for my own good, but why? I study A.J.'s broad back and try to guess at his intentions. Victor's at his side, handing off something to another kid while A.J. blocks them with his body. "Fighter" is the word that comes to mind. It's in his posture, the way he keeps his head low, arms at his sides, ready. He turns then and catches my eye. I look away to find Margo watching us.

"He's so totally into you," she says, and clasps her hands over her heart in a faux swoon.

"No, he's not. He just *glared* at me."

"That was not a glare, my friend. That was hot. That look was saturated with primal lust and longing."

I laugh. "Whatever you say, Margo."

She offers me her box of Tic Tacs, and I drop a couple on my tongue—sweet, citrusy sunshine. "A.J.'s a good guy," she says, taking a few Tic Tacs for herself. "But he's not always a *nice* guy."

"What's the difference?"

"Nice guys do what you tell them to. Good guys do what's right."

Important to know, I guess. But I'm not looking for a guy, nice or not. I'm looking for a way out.

CHAPTER 4

After school I report to the dorms for "group activities," which means all the girls from the third floor crowd into the common room to watch a "motivational" film. The room reeks of Secret deodorant and bad breath. Kayla shuts out the lights, and I go stand in the back of the room where it's easier to breathe. Charlotte's there already and glances over at me nervously. I back up in case she needs more space.

Kayla starts the movie, and it opens up with this man—Craig—playing fetch with a golden retriever on a massive TruGreen lawn behind a fancy house. Craig starts talking about how he used to be an alcoholic and how it got so bad that he lost his job and house and had to live on the streets. The film flashes to what's supposed to be a dramatization of Craig as a homeless guy, then flashes back to present-day Craig on the lawn, scratching the dog's chin as he launches into this revival speech on how he owes all his "financial success" and "emotional security" to the program.

AA, that is.

My mom went through Alcoholics Anonymous after she

and my dad split, and I went with her to meetings. I'd sit in a corner and do my homework while they had group. There was a lot of hugging and crying and talking. I tried not to listen, because it wasn't my business, but I believed those meetings would keep my mom sober. For a while, they did.

I remember trying to convince my mom to go to a meeting one time, after she'd gone on a really bad drinking binge and wrecked her car, but she said she couldn't face them. Because they looked up to her, and she didn't want them to see how she'd failed.

And here's Craig, the success story, who seems to have shed all those years of alcoholism like a too-small coat. He doesn't act like any of the alcoholics I've known, recovering or not. He's too cheesy and too . . . self-righteous. I don't believe Craig has ever seen the bleak hopelessness of addiction, because if he had, then maybe he wouldn't be so cheery about it.

Then I think, he's probably just an actor playing an alcoholic on TV. I'm being lied to. We all are.

The video ends, and Kayla flips on the lights and asks us questions like, "How do we feel empowered by Craig's story?" and "How can we apply Craig's winning attitude to our own lives?"

I keep quiet. I'm not the only one.

Then she passes out worksheets for us to fill out, asking us to be "open and honest" with our responses. I scan the questions.

Have you ever experimented with drugs or alcohol?

Which ones? How many? How often?

How did it make you feel?

All I can think to write is "None of your business," but I know that won't fly, so I just sit down in the corner of the room with my head in my arms and pretend to be asleep.

"Participation is the first step to rehabilitation," Kayla says tartly as she collects my blank worksheet.

After group we have "leisure," a fancy word for lazing around. Most everyone else drifts out, so I stay in the common room and get comfortable on the couch. *Judge Judy*'s on TV. My mom and I are big fans of Judge Judy. She cuts right through the bull and doesn't put up with a lot of drama in the courtroom, even though they seem to bring in the least rational people they can find. That's entertainment.

Judge Judy's in the middle of giving the business to this guy who'd accepted money for painting a house but then never finished the job, when I realize I'm alone in the room. A bad feeling washes over me as I glance left, then right. The Latina Queens. I scramble up off the couch. Someone yanks my hair so hard my neck pops. When I open up my mouth to scream, they stuff a gag in it.

They push me back on the couch and pile on top of me as I kick and thrash against them. I manage a garbled scream before they shove my face into the musty couch cushion.

Someone climbs on my back, digging their bony knees into my spine. I'm powerless to stop them, doing everything I can to just breathe. I wrench one arm free and swing blindly, connecting with some girl's face.

"Bitch," she utters, and falls back.

I'm about to grab for someone else when all of a sudden, they're gone. I look around to find myself alone in the common room. I draw a few ragged breaths and push the gag out with my tongue. It's somebody's disgusting sock.

I flex my hand, and my fingers brush against something soft and animal-like. I glance down at a long serpentine tail lying next to me on the couch.

Not a tail. A black braid.

My hair.

Next to it are the scissors from Mr. Chris's class. The scissors *she* stole. I reach behind me to feel only the stubby ends of my hair, which now end right at my neck.

They cut off all my hair.

I grab the scissors and my braid and storm out to the hallway, heading straight for Brandi's room, but Tracy cuts me off. She comes out of nowhere and gets right up in my face, so close I can smell the Fritos on her breath. "What's going on here?" she demands.

"Taylor, what'd you do?" Kayla says, closing in from behind.

I'm trapped between them. I have the urge to shove Tracy

out of the way, but she's huge, and I know there will be consequences. I feel as though I've been punched in the gut. All
I can do now is tattle on them, something I hate doing.

"They did it," I say to Tracy, and hold up my braid as proof.
"In the common room. They cut off my hair."

"Who?" Kayla asks.

"Brandi and her *gang*."

Kayla frowns a little, denting the space between her eyebrows. "Brandi," she calls.

Brandi appears in her doorway with a perfect poker face.

"Brandi, is this true?"

"Is what true?" she says oh-so-innocently.

"Did you cut Taylor's hair?"

She looks at me like it hurts her feelings that I would
accuse her of such a thing. "No, ma'am. I was just in my room
listening to music with Trish."

On cue, Trish appears in the doorway with one earbud in
her ear. She holds the other one out like it's meant for Brandi.

"Aren't those the sharps from Mr. Chris's class?" Trish says,
pointing to the scissors in my fist. She's reading a line they've
already rehearsed. I squeeze the scissors with all my strength.
I can't believe this is happening.

"That's right. Didn't they find them in her backpack?"
Brandi says.

"Taylor, where'd you get those?" Kayla asks me.

I can't look at her or even speak. I'm so angry that they're getting away with this. Then I see Charlotte standing in her doorway. Her room has a clear view of the common room and the couch. She must have seen something.

"You saw them," I say to Charlotte. "You saw what they did, didn't you?"

She looks at me like a scared rabbit, but I know it's not me she's afraid of. It's them.

"Charlotte, did you see what happened?" Kayla asks.

"I was coloring." She turns toward me. "It doesn't look that bad."

"Give me the scissors," Tracy says, and I force myself to hand them over calmly. "Stay in your room until dinner."

I don't trust myself not to give Brandi and Trish a righteous stiff-arm, so I walk straight past them without looking up. In my room I scream into my pillow and pound the mattress with both fists.

When my anger subsides, I glance up to see my comb lying on the bureau and figure I won't be needing it anymore. I pick it up, turn it over in my hands, then use the edge of the bureau to snap off its teeth, one after the other. I think again of Andy the security guard. He liked to drink, but he wasn't an alcoholic, which is why he and my mom eventually broke up. My mom's pretty good at faking sobriety, but never for very long.

Anyway, one time Andy was over at our house kicking back

a few when he decided to teach me and my mom some basic self-defense moves. It was all in all pretty hilarious, but the thing I remembered was that he used a sharpened pencil to show us how to attack. You could stab someone in the side of the neck, or for a direct hit, aim for the eyeball. If your assailant's arms get in the way, stab them in the side, thrusting upward so the pencil gets under the rib cage and punctures something important.

I retrieve Margo's matches from my backpack. With my back to the door, I light one, using the flame to melt the plastic into a fine, sharp point.

"Hey."

A voice. A *guy's* voice. In my room. I jump to my feet and survey the room in one fast sweep.

"You there?" he asks.

I open the closet and look under the bed, the only places he could hide, but I'm alone in the room. Then I realize his voice is coming from the air vent, same as the guitar.

"I heard screaming."

It never occurred to me that if I could hear into someone else's room, they might also be able to hear into mine. I glance out to the hallway—clear—then drop down on my hands and knees over the vent.

"That was me," I say, "but it was . . . nothing." Not nothing, but nothing I can explain through an air vent to a perfect stranger.

"So, you're . . . okay?"

I notice his accent, a slight twang. Not like some of the other kids' exaggerated drawls. More like a slow pour, like there's no rush for words.

"Yeah, I'm fine." I pause for a moment, thinking it's pretty considerate of him to ask, but also weird and slightly creepy that he can hear into my room at any time of day.

"Who are you?" I ask, but he doesn't respond. Maybe he didn't hear me or maybe he left the room. I sit back and wait for him to say something else, but there is nothing.

A few minutes later Kayla comes into my room and asks me what happened with my hair and the scissors, so I tell her. Again. She says she's going to set up peer mediation between Brandi and me, which just sounds like more punishment, so I change my story and tell her I cut my hair myself.

"You're sure that's the truth?" Kayla asks.

"Does it even matter?"

"Of course it matters, Taylor. If Brandi did it, then she needs to admit to it and try to make it up to you."

"Can she bring back my hair?"

"Well . . . no."

"Then I don't want to talk about it anymore."

But she keeps asking me to tell her what *really* happened. So I sit there—still as a stone—until she throws up her hands in frustration and a safety calls our floor to dinner.

Downstairs I tell Margo the true story of my run-in with the Latina Queens. My hair keeps falling in my face, irritating me, and I keep having to push it out of my eyes, since it's now too short to pull back into a ponytail.

"The thing that really gets me," I say to her over a slice of mystery meat and gritty mashed potatoes, "is that they were all in on it together. Even Charlotte saw what happened and didn't say anything."

Margo shakes her head. "Don't take it personal, T. The Latina Queens rule the third floor. It's the law of the jungle up there—eat or get eaten. Be the predator or be the prey."

"I thought people here were supposed to be happy. Everyone in the brochure is smiling."

Margo laughs. "Those are just models. Unattractive ones. But you're better off than me. The girls on my floor are always cutting themselves with paper clips and accusing me of stealing things."

"Stealing things? What things?"

She doesn't answer me; she does that a lot. "Don't worry about the Latina Queens. I'll get them back for you. I'm kind of the expert at that."

"How?"

Margo winks. "Don't you worry your pretty little head about it."

We finish with our dinner and dump our trays—cardboard,

plasticware and all. I get this crazy impulse to jump into the garbage can and hide there until I get thrown out, eventually re-emerging at a landfill far, far away.

"Hustle your bustle," Margo says. "I want us to get good seats for the show."

I follow her into the media center, which is just this huge room with rows and rows of chairs with a podium in the front and a big-screen projector where they show movies and PowerPoint presentations. Last night the topic was teen suicide. Tonight it's eating disorders. By "good seats," Margo means the back row, where Victor's saved us two spots between him and A.J. A.J. glances up at my hair, which I'm sure looks like crap. I reach back to try and fix it, but it can't be helped.

"Where's the popcorn?" Victor asks Margo.

"There were mice in the popcorn," Margo says, "and the soda machine was out of order. I hope you brought the candy."

Victor opens his jacket wide enough to reveal a bag of M&M's, and she claps her hands with delight. The lights dim, and the movie begins with a doctor talking about the importance of a healthy body image. Margo and Victor break into the candy, and we pass it among us. It's been a while since I've had any real junk food and I don't want to lose it, so I'm careful to keep it out of sight. When I glance over at Margo and Victor, they're holding hands and whispering to each other. Every once in a while, Victor steals a kiss. It's sweet and kind of sad, too, that this is probably the closest they get to going out on a date.

I glance over at A.J., who's leaned back in his chair with his arms crossed, a thoughtful expression on his face. I wonder what he's thinking right now. I hardly ever see him with anyone but Victor. I wonder what he did to wind up in a place like Sunny Meadows, but that's not the sort of thing you ask someone you hardly know. Unless, of course, you're Margo Blanchard.

I don't realize I'm still staring until A.J. glances over at me. His gaze drifts from my eyes to my hair, and I suddenly feel hot and embarrassed.

"I didn't cut it myself," I say, then feel like an idiot. "My hair, I mean."

I don't know why I feel the need to tell him that. Maybe because of the rumors circulating at dinner, about how the new girl on the third floor went berserk and cut off her own hair. He probably doesn't even care, but I want him to know the truth.

He nods like he gets it, but doesn't say anything. Maybe he's afraid of getting in trouble with the safeties, but I don't think it's a big deal to talk, since most everyone else is talking by now. Or maybe it's one of those things where he doesn't want to be rude by ignoring me, but also doesn't want me to keep on talking.

I face forward for the rest of the presentation. The lights come on, and the interns all stand at the front of the room taking turns trying to get us to spill our guts. There are a few people who reliably will, which is good because if they keep talking, the rest of us don't have to. When the Q&A is over, people get up to leave, and I overhear Victor tell Margo he's putting in an order tomorrow.

"Do you ladies need anything?"

"I do," I pipe up. I don't know how much it will cost me, but I'm sure it will be worth it.

"What is it?"

"A road map of Georgia."

"What for?" Margo says suspiciously.

"School project," I lie. "The Revolutionary War."

"Why can't you just get a map from class?"

Good question . . . why can't I?

"Because none of the maps are—detailed enough."

"Why would you need a detailed map?"

I look at her. I didn't expect the third degree, and I have no other answer but the truth, that I'm planning my escape and need to know where the heck I'm going.

"Never mind."

"Because getting a map of Georgia sounds like a really *bad* idea."

Victor glances from me to Margo, like he doesn't want

to interfere, while A.J. studies me closely, trying to read me. I focus my eyes on the back of the chair in front of me. I should have known better than to ask them for anything. I have to do this on my own, in complete secrecy, if my plan is going to work. Out of the corner of my eye I see Margo cross her arms. I can tell she's miffed.

"Let us know if you change your mind," Victor says to me, and then to Margo, *"Bonne nuit, ma chérie."*

They leave with the rest of the guys, and Margo turns to me. "Why do you need a map of Georgia?"

"You were right, Margo, it's a bad idea."

"Are you just saying that or do you really mean it?"

I don't answer her, and she lets it go for about five seconds. "As your peer mentor, I'm advising you to pick a *different* school project."

Our interns call us over, and Margo lines up with the girls from the second floor. I'm suddenly worried she might tell on me. But it's not like I've done anything wrong. Still, I don't want the safeties poking through my stuff. I need to find a better hiding place for my money, just in case they decide to search my bags again.

I follow the third-floor girls through the lobby and catch a glimpse of the night outside the glass doors. They probably keep the doors locked at night, but there's only one safety manning the lobby. If I could sneak down here after lights-out . . .

When I get to my room, I look around for a better hiding place for my money. The bed is too obvious, since all they'd have to do is strip the sheets. If I had some tape, I could attach it to the inside of the dresser. My eyes rove over the air vent, and I get an idea. Maybe I could wedge my money between the grate and the floor. I kneel before it and hook my fingernails under the metal.

"You there?"

I'm so startled by his voice that I fall back on my butt. It takes me a couple of seconds to recover. He can't see me, though, can he?

"I'm here," I say.

"You want to get off your floor?"

It's as if he read my mind. I glance out to the hallway to make sure no one else is listening.

"Yeah, I do," I say, "but I can't."

"Sure you can," he says, taunting me.

"Can anyone else hear us?"

"I don't know. Let's make this quick. Meet me tonight after lights-out. In the basement."

"What? Are you insane?"

"Don't you want to sneak out?"

I didn't know sneaking out was a possibility. Margo never said anything to me about sneaking out. And she would know.

"How would I?" I ask. Not that I'd do it, but because I'm curious to know.

"Go down the stairwell between the dorms."

The stairwell between the boys' and girls' dorms, behind door number one.

"It's locked."

"I have a key. I'll unlock it from my side."

A key to the locked stairwell door? I can hardly believe it. A key exists, and he has one.

"Where'd you get the key?" I ask him.

"Come down and I'll tell you."

I rock back on my heels. He's baiting me, and the bait is good. He might be crazy. He might want to harm me, but if he has a key to the stairwell, he might have keys to other places too. He seems like someone I should know.

"Who are you?" I ask, but what follows is a long silence. Unlike the last time I asked him, this time I know he heard me.

"Go all the way down," he says at last. "Turn into the third door on the right. You're not afraid of the dark, are you?"

I stop and think. Am I afraid of the dark? Not when I'm alone, like here in my room, but with a stranger—a strange guy? Maybe. Why does it have to be dark at all? What if this is a trap?

"No, I'm not."

"So, you'll come down?"

I could get caught by Sandra, the night safety, or one of the other girls, which means getting thrown into a time-out room. He might be some safety creep who lures girls down to the basement to rape and murder them. Or he could be just your average Sunny Meadows psychopath. The risk is high, but getting off the floor at night is the first step to getting out of this place. I can bring my sharpened comb. The potential payoff is pretty huge.

"I'll be there," I tell him.

"All right. See you then."

I stand and stretch my legs, then stuff my money into one pocket and Tatters into the other. Just in case the opportunity arises. I glance at the digital clock on the dresser. Forty-five minutes until lights-out. In less than an hour, I could be free.

CHAPTER 5

I wait until Sandra makes her rounds, then creep silently to my doorway and peek across the hall to where Brandi is asleep in her bed, snoring softly with her mouth partway open. Slowly, noiselessly, I pick up one of my duffel bags and lay it across my bed, pulling up the covers and arranging it to look like a body, just in case Sandra does a room check. It takes forever to do it, measuring each movement so that it goes unnoticed. I grab my comb dagger from under my pillow, take a deep breath, and pad out into the hallway on bare feet, aiming for the stairwell door, which thankfully is catty-corner to my own.

I remember the last time I tried the door and found it locked. Maybe the voice in the vent is lying to me about the key. Or maybe it's a trick and there's a safety waiting on the other side, ready to bust me.

I push down on the metal bar and ease the door open. I wait for an alarm to sound but there is nothing, save for the rapid beating of my own heart. When the door closes behind me, it sounds like a tomb sealing shut. I grab the handrail to steady myself and follow the stairs down into the black belly of the dorms.

The basement is dark, except for the glowing red EXIT sign. I head there first and push down on the metal bar. Locked. But maybe he has the key to this door too. If I could get out of the dorms at night, I could climb the fence and make a run for the road, hitch a ride, and be long gone by morning.

I double back and find the third door on the right, our designated meeting place. What remains of my courage swiftly evaporates as I turn the knob and enter into total, blind darkness. I feel my way along a narrow passageway, which turns a sharp corner and seems to open up into a slightly larger space. The air smells like vinegar and moth-balls, dank and heavy. I grip my comb tighter and rehearse the hard, jabbing motion Andy taught me years ago.

I trace along the wall with my fingertips until I find the light switch. I flip it on, but nothing happens. I flip it again. And again.

"It's a darkroom."

I jump at the sound of his voice; it's so deep I feel the vibrations in my gut. My legs are weak and rubbery as I pivot slowly and try to determine exactly where he stands.

"For photographs," he says.

"It's really dark," I say, an obvious statement, but it *is* really dark.

"I unscrewed the lightbulbs."

I take a step back, my feet itching to run back the way I came. "Why would you do that?"

"In case you get caught. I don't want them to know who got you off the floor."

"I wouldn't rat you out."

"How do I know for sure?"

The dare in his voice makes me want to argue further, but I understand his logic. It's something I myself would do. But to be this close to him, without knowing his name or what he looks like—I'm at a definite disadvantage.

"Are you a safety?" I ask.

He laughs. "No."

"Do you know who I am?"

"You're the new girl."

The new girl. My dorm room must have been empty before I got here. Or not. What if he murdered the last girl? What if I just stepped into a real-life horror movie?

"I'm not going to hurt you," he says, as though sensing my fear. He may as well have said, *I'm not going to murder you,* for all the good it does me. But I hear him moving away, and the next time he speaks, it's from across the room.

"There's a couch ten steps in front of you, if you want to sit."

The idea of sitting down next to him, where he can reach out and grab me, does nothing to calm my nerves, especially after my last misfortune involving a couch. "I'm good here," I say, and wait for my eyes to adjust to the dark. I shut them and open them again—absolutely no difference.

"Have we met?" I say. "I mean, are you in one of my classes?"

"I'm not going to give myself away."

That's exactly what I was hoping he would do, but I guess it doesn't matter. I'm not going to make a habit of meeting him here like this. I just wanted to see if it could be done. And it can. But not without him. And not without his key.

"How'd you get that key?"

He chuckles. There's nothing funny as far as I can tell. "Is that the only reason you came?"

"Why else would I come?"

"I thought you might want to see me."

"But I can't see you."

"Hmm, I guess not. Why do you care so much about the key?"

I can't tell him the real reason, that I'm trying to run away. And I can't think of any other excuse that wouldn't be completely transparent.

"I'm just curious."

He's silent for a moment, then says, "I'll tell you, but you have to tell me something about yourself first."

"Why?" I don't know anything about him, but he wants to

know more about me. I'm the new girl, and that's all there is to know.

"I'm just curious," he says, throwing my words back at me. "But I'll make it easy for you. Tell me . . . what you had for dinner."

Dinner? What a weird question. I can hardly remember.

"Some kind of meat. It was salty and mushy—I don't think it was real—and mashed potatoes, instant ones. I bit into a part that hadn't gotten mixed with water. It was pretty gross, actually."

"Sounds like it."

"Your turn," I say, not losing sight of my mission. "Where'd you get the key?"

"I know a locksmith on the outside."

"So you just—took it?"

"Ah, now it's your turn again."

I clench my jaw.

"Who do you miss the most?" he says.

"What do you mean?"

"From your life before Sunny Meadows. Who do you miss?"

"My grandmother." I say it without hesitation, without even having to think about it. My answer surprises me. My grandmother's been dead for six years.

"What do you miss about her?"

"It's your turn," I remind him. I didn't make up the rules, but I catch on quickly.

"I borrowed the janitor's keys to open the school gym," he says. "I made a mold of the key."

"How did you make it?"

"What do you miss about your grandmother?"

I really don't want to talk about her, with him or anyone else. There is so much to miss—her voice, her hands, the smell of her kitchen, her stories and songs, all the games we used to play. I miss just being around her.

"Her garden," I say. "It's where I felt the most . . . calm." I think about the summers we spent together—long, hot days that stretched on without beginning or end, all the time we spent outside pulling weeds, eating vegetables right from the ground, living on fresh air and sunshine. But that was a long time ago, and I'll never get that feeling back. Not without her.

"How do you make the mold?" I ask him.

"I press the key into something soft, like plaster, something that holds the shape. It costs extra to do it that way, but it works. Most of the time."

"How many keys do you have?"

"What'd you do to get into Sunny Meadows?"

My defenses go up like a wall around me. "What did *you* do?"

Silence is what follows. It seems this is a question neither of us wants to answer.

"I really just want to know about the key," I say at last. "I didn't know this was going to be an exposé on all the things that are none of your business."

"A few."

"A few what?"

"I have a few keys."

"What about the basement door?"

"Why would you need that key?"

"So I can go for a walk outside. You could come too. Wouldn't that be nice?"

He chuckles. "Is it because of a guy? You trying to meet up with your boyfriend?"

I snort. "Not quite."

"Well, if you're not running *to* someone, then you must be running *from* someone . . . or something."

"Is this therapy? Are you playing psychologist or just doing it to piss me off?" My anger throbs like a fever. I need to move, but I can't see *anything*.

"I'm not trying to be your therapist," he says, "and I don't have a key to the basement."

"Could you get one?"

"I don't know. I've never tried."

"Why not?" What good is a key to the stairwell if it only leads to the basement? Maybe he has one and he's lying about it. Maybe he's afraid I'll figure out who he is and tell on him.

"Because I'm not trying to go for a walk outside," he says tensely. "One more question and then we're done. Better make it good."

One more question. What should I be asking him? What more is there to know?

"Where do you keep your keys?" I say, then add, "So the safeties don't find them."

It's an obvious question, and he probably knows why I'm asking it, but he also seems cocky enough to answer me. But instead he's moving across the room, coming closer and closer until he's right in front of me. Definitely *within* reach. Maybe he has night-vision goggles, too.

"Do you think you could get them?" he says. He's so close I can feel his voice in my bones and the heat coming off his body. His sharp, piney scent reminds me of the woods behind my grandmother's house.

"Maybe I could," I say, fighting to keep my voice from quaking.

"I keep them *real close*," he says, and then he's moving again, circling around until he's standing right behind me.

But I don't wait to see what he does next.

I dart away, scrambling sideways like a crab, and follow the hallway out of the darkroom. I stumble up the stairs and don't stop until I'm back in my bedroom on the third floor, where I stand in the middle of my room, breathing hard.

After my fear and adrenaline fade and my brain starts working again, I know one thing for certain: I have to figure out who he is.

I have to get those keys.

CHAPTER 6

The next morning I stand in front of my smeary mirror and inspect my hair, which hasn't just been cut, it has been severed, with loose strands dangling down and a strange slant going from one side to the other. I could probably convince Kayla to let me borrow some scissors to fix it, but that would feel too much like giving in.

Unable to do anything about my hair, I review the facts about my mystery man in the basement. Judging by our closer encounters, I figure he's a good bit taller than me. Deep voice with a Southern accent, although accents can be faked. I'd say he probably likes to talk a lot too. Fairly smart and very sneaky.

Really, his voice is the best thing I have to go on. All I have to do is hear him talk and I'll know. But if he wants to remain anonymous, he won't talk to me or within my earshot. I need to be listening without *appearing* to be listening.

During walkover, I spy on the boys' line to see if any of them are looking my way. A few of them are, but it doesn't really count because I'm already staring at them like a crazy stalker.

In first period, Mr. Chris passes out worksheets on American Revolutionaries like Paul Revere and the notorious traitor Benedict Arnold. Sulli's my partner for the assignment, but instead of helping me answer questions, he's retelling that stupid rumor—the one where I'm the psycho and the Latina Queens are the victims of my homicidal rage, which by now feels like old news.

"So that's why you stole that sharp," Sulli says to me, like he's Sherlock Holmes having an *aha* moment.

"Your psycho girlfriend stole the sharp," I say, glaring at Brandi's back because I know she's listening. "And you can tell her I'm going to get her back. If I'm lucky, it'll be bad enough to get me kicked out of this place."

"I like it," he says, reaching over to pick up a piece of my hair, letting it drop against my cheek. "Short and *sexy*."

"*Don't* touch me." I scoot my desk back to where it was before we teamed up—I'll finish this assignment myself. I'm fairly certain Sulli is *not* my man in the basement, unless he's incredibly good at faking accents. I stop and listen to the voices of the guys all around me, but it's impossible to get a good read with everyone talking at once.

First period ends, and I continue my search in Algebra II and English, but no likely suspects surface. By lunchtime I'm ready to tell Margo about my secret meeting, if only to see whether she might have a lead. But then I'd have to tell her about the key. And if people find out there's a key to the stairwell door, the safeties will come looking for it, and it might be lost to me forever.

I have to think long-term.

We stroll out to the pen, and Margo walks over to Victor, who is standing, as always, with A.J. I follow her over even though it's a little weird, the way *they're* always together and *we're* always together, like some forced double date.

I stand off to the side while Margo pretends to be flirting with Victor, but really she's narrating the girls' orders in French. From what Margo has told me before, they're mostly candy and cosmetics. Nothing gets written down. Not included on their list is one road map of Georgia, but I'm not bitter. I gather from this exchange that Margo is the girls' liaison for their smuggling ring, and she takes orders from everyone *except* the Latina Queens, which might be part of the reason they hate her. I'm still not sure about A.J.'s role in this operation. Then I realize I haven't yet profiled him. I glance at him sideways. He's big enough, but I'd need to hear his voice to know for sure.

"Pretty sunny today," I say to him. The weather isn't much of a talking point. It's always sunny here. Sunny, Sunny Meadows.

He indulges me by squinting up at the sky and nodding his head in agreement. But he still doesn't speak.

"How was your lunch?" I ask. He shrugs and makes an icky face. "I think I ate an armadillo, or maybe it was a bilge rat. Very gamey."

He smiles at my weak attempt at humor. He looks almost friendly when he smiles, but why won't he talk to me? I need a question he can't dodge or answer yes or no to.

"I've got automotive next. How about you?"

He stares at me, in my eyes, so deep and penetrating I forget I'm waiting for an answer.

Victor taps him on the shoulder. "Onward and upward, my friend."

A.J. nods once at me and turns away. I grab Margo by her elbow. "Why won't he talk to me?"

"Who?"

"A.J."

"He doesn't talk to anyone."

"What?"

"I thought you knew that."

I stare after him. He doesn't talk to anyone? "Why not?" I ask her.

She shrugs. "He used to talk when he first got here. Then one day he just—stopped."

The bell rings, and I watch A.J. pass by us on his way inside. He gives me an almost smile and I return it. I want to know what made him stop talking. I realize that makes him an unlikely candidate for my basement friend, but just because he *chooses* not to talk doesn't mean he can't. I won't cross him off the list just yet.

I continue on to automotive therapy, which is my only elective class. All the electives here have a therapy twist to them—art therapy, dance therapy, team sports therapy, woodshop therapy, and on and on. I figure with automotive, I'll at least have access to cars, even if we're not allowed to drive them. I know because I asked the guidance counselor when he was signing me up. "*No driving*," he said, and made sure I heard him.

I walk into class that afternoon for the first time to find twenty guys in their undershirts, two other girls, and no Latina Queens. I could do a lot worse.

The garage smells like car oil and grease rags and a bunch of sweaty dudes, but I kind of like it. It reminds me of the warehouse, and with all these guys in close quarters I have a good chance of finding my mystery man. For the first few minutes I stand there with my eyes half-closed, listening to them talk, trying to find a match.

Several of the guys have Southern accents, but none seem to fit just right. And the harder I concentrate, the more unsure I am of what his voice really sounds like. It isn't the same alone in the dark as it is in the daytime with all these other people around.

Frustrated, I turn my attention to phase two of my getaway plan: mode of transportation. Hitching a ride is one option, but not a very desirable one. Even better than being a passenger is being the driver.

There's an old Ford Bronco and a Toyota Camry parked in the four-car garage, but the teacher, Mr. Thomas, keeps a tight watch on the keys. And even if I could slip them away, neither of the cars is running. At least, not yet.

Mr. Thomas tells me the first thing I'll be learning is how to change a flat tire. He partners me up with this guy Dominic, who has a tattoo of a Chinese dragon that starts at his elbow and curves up to his shoulder. It's a beautiful tattoo, with all the tiny scales shaded differently to show how the dragon's body bends and twists.

"Nice tat," I say to him. It's an easy opener.

He glances down and admires it himself for a moment. "Thanks."

One word and I know Dominic is not my man. But he turns out to be pretty cool. He gives me pointers on how to position my body to get the most leverage while jacking up the car and loosening the lug nuts. Then, while we're switching out the tires, we start talking about music. Turns out he's seen Choleric Kindness play out in Atlanta. He tells me about where he's from, how he got involved with drugs and messed up his relationship with his family and his girlfriend.

His parents sent him here to sober up, and he says when he gets out in December, the first thing he's going to do is try to make it up to them.

Class flies by way too fast. After school is my first therapy appointment at the "healing center." After about ten minutes of waiting, I get called in. I glance over at the therapist—Dr. Deb—and take a look around her office. At least it smells good in here, like peppermint, and there are potted plants lining the sills of actual windows where you can see the world outside. I sit down across from Dr. Deb in a wing-backed chair. We're close, but not too close. She looks friendly, but not overly friendly—not as if she cares if I like her or not. She introduces herself as my primary therapist and asks how my first few days have been.

"Decent," I say, and hope she'll leave it at that.

"Are you making friends?"

"Yeah," I say. Margo feels like a friend already.

"Are you getting along with the girls on your floor?"

I wonder then if she's already been briefed about the hair-cutting incident—maybe by Kayla—and if so, what version she's been told.

"More or less."

"Is there anything you'd like to talk about in that regard?"

I meet her eyes squarely. "No."

"You're sure?"

"Yep." It's not like there's anything she can do about it, even if she did believe me.

"Then why don't you tell me about where you come from," she says, "beginning with your family."

My family. Not a subject I want to discuss.

"I have a mother and a father," I say neutrally.

"Are they divorced?"

"Separated."

"And you were living with your mother at the time you ran away?"

"Yes." The questions are getting harder already.

"Were you going to your father's house?"

"No."

"Why not?"

Why not? Why would I?

"My father and I don't get along."

"Why is that?"

"I don't know."

"Is he abusive?"

"No, just . . . controlling."

"Controlling. Could you give me an example?"

"He sent me here, didn't he?"

Dr. Deb nods. "You think that was his attempt to control you?"

I think back to earlier this year, June, which was the last

time I tried to spend the weekend at his house. The school had just mailed out my report card, and it wasn't too great. I mean, it was pretty good considering how bad the year had been. But he still flipped out on me and told me I was grounded for the weekend. Grounded, after I'd basically been taking care of myself that whole year. My mother, too. So I waited for him to go do something in the other room, then walked out of his house and called a friend to come pick me up. Boy, was he mad at that.

Still, I never thought he'd do this.

"Can you remember a time when your relationship with your father was stronger than it is now?" Dr. Deb asks.

"No. Not since he left my mom."

"Why don't you tell me about it?"

"About what?"

"Tell me about their separation."

I was in fifth grade when my parents split for good. I'd just come home from school, and I was inside having a snack when my mom came back. When I saw her, I no longer cared that she'd totally left us for a week or that we had no idea where she went or when she'd be back, *if* she'd be back. I was so happy to see her I forgot about the entire week of worrying.

My dad told me to stay inside, and he went out on the lawn to talk to her. It turned into a fight, something I always hated—seeing them screaming at each other. I didn't understand why they were fighting at all. I just wanted him to let her inside so we could get back to being a family.

She stood on the lawn apologizing, pleading with him. When I ran outside, he told me to get back in the house, but I clung to her. She was my life raft, my mother. She needed me and I needed her. My dad got into his car and told me to come with him. I wouldn't, so he drove off. My mother and I went inside and packed our things, then left in her car. I wanted to stay, but she didn't. She said it was going to be a new beginning for us. *An exciting adventure.* And it was . . . for a while.

"He's mad at me for choosing her," I say to Dr. Deb.

"For choosing to live with your mother?"

"Yes."

"You think he's still mad at you for that?"

"I don't know. Do we have to talk about this?"

"Is there something else you'd rather talk about?"

"I'd rather not talk at all."

"Okay."

We sit there in silence. I watch the hands on the clock move by infinitesimal degrees. I can't get that memory out of my head. My parents' faces, so twisted up with anger they were like total strangers. Me standing between them. I don't want to dredge up those feelings. I just want them to go away.

"Why did you run away, Taylor?"

"I thought we weren't going to talk."

"I'm just asking questions. I'm trying to learn your side of the story."

Why did I run away? It isn't the right question. The right question is, why didn't I run away sooner? Why didn't I have a plan? Why didn't I do a better job of disappearing?

"I don't know," I say finally.

"What were you doing when you made the decision to run away?"

I think back to a few weeks ago. It was a weeknight and it was hot, too, I remember, because the AC wasn't working. But my mom didn't want to call the landlord to fix it because we were late on the rent, which was pretty standard by then.

"I was on my way to the bathroom," I say to Dr. Deb.

It was the middle of the night, and I had to go pee. I came out of my room and tripped over this guy who was passed out in our hallway, some sleaze my mom brought home from the bar. I'd heard them laughing earlier that night, and I'd just locked my door and gone to bed, figuring he'd be gone by the time I got up, which was usually the case. But there he was, lying in my hallway, fat and bloated and disgusting, while my mom was passed out in her own bedroom across the hall.

"What happened to make you want to run away, Taylor?"

It wasn't what happened. It was what didn't happen. It was like everything came crashing down then. I could no longer pretend that she was going to stop drinking, that she'd wake up the next day and decide to change. She wasn't even trying to hide it anymore. She gave up on sobriety and she gave up on me.

"I just wanted out of there," I say at last.

"Out of where?"

"Out of our apartment, out of my life. I wanted *out*."

I taste the memory in my mouth, like sour oranges, and it makes me sick. I don't want to go back there.

"How did you feel in that moment, Taylor? Right before you ran?"

But I can't answer her, because the feeling is rising— stronger and faster than ever before. I feel the fist squeezing me, cutting off my air. My heart's pounding and my mouth goes dry and I have to get out of there. I have to just *go*.

I jump up and run out of her office, tearing down the hallways as fast as I can, right past the safety manning the door. When I get outside, my face hits the sunshine, my shoes hit the grass, and I'm running. Running for my life. I sprint away from the healing center as fast as I can. It feels so good to blur everything around me, leave everything behind, and focus only on what's in front of me. After a few more strides, my chest opens up and I can breathe again.

"Stop!" a safety shouts. I fly right by him, past the soccer field and the maintenance shed. Seconds later I hit the back fence and grab hold of it, shaking it with both hands until the metal bites into my fingers. Another safety comes up on my side and I run the other way, pumping my legs as hard as I can. I'm not going to stop, for him or anyone else. I feel so good in that moment, so free. I could run forever.

That's when the safety's arm appears out of nowhere.

With superhuman strength he clotheslines me in the chest. My feet fly up, my back hits the dirt, and my head smacks the ground with a tremendous thud. My eyes roll back into my head and snap wide open.

I stare up in a daze at the ultrabright, cerulean sky.

CHAPTER 7

I'm lying there in the grass with my throbbing head and aching chest when the laughing begins. It erupts from my gut with volcanic force. I can't stop it. I can't control it. I'm so shocked by the force of his takedown that I laugh, like a maniac, while the safeties stand over me like sweaty, red-faced devils. It's the same thing I did when the cops caught up with me, but I can't explain that to them. I can barely breathe. Besides, I don't think they care.

They haul me to my feet and drag me up the hill. I laugh. They take me into the first floor and shut me in a time-out room, and my laughter escalates to semi-hysteria. I lie down on the cold, hard floor and grip my cramping stomach, trying to calm down, trying to breathe.

Finally the laughing gives way to spontaneous giggles, then a steady *he, he, he* and at last, hiccups. I wipe the tears from my eyes and roll over onto my back.

Now I'm angry.

That a grown man tackled me—roughly, even by boy standards—and they stuck me in here just for running. I want to smash something, but there's only a toilet, a sink, and a metal chair, all bolted to the floor. There's nothing I can break, throw, or pound, except something of my own, and I'm too damn sore for that. Plus, there's a safety outside the door, watching me through the reinforced glass, and a camera behind a cage documenting it all.

I think back to when I was nine years old and this police officer came up to my car door window, asking me where my mom was. My dad was out of town, and we were parked outside a bar because she needed to get some money from a friend inside, but she'd been in there for a while—two hours at least. I should have just gone inside and gotten her myself, but I'd never been to this place before, and I figured if I just waited long enough, she'd eventually come back out.

I didn't want to answer the officer's questions, but he promised me my mom wasn't going to be in trouble, so finally I told him. The next thing I know they've got my mom in handcuffs, and they're stuffing her into a police cruiser while I scream and fight with them. All I want is to go with her, wherever they're taking her, I don't care, just let me go. But I can't because that same lying cop is holding me back.

I spent the night on a cot in a complete stranger's house, in a room crowded with kids, one of whom spent the whole night wheezing and moaning. I can still smell that room—like Cheez-Its and dirty diapers. It was a night I'll never forget.

I've got to get out of here.

I stare up at the one fluorescent light, at the moth pinging into it, over and over again, trying to . . . I have no idea what it's trying to do, but I feel like that moth, ramming my head against an invisible wall, getting nothing from it but a wicked headache.

My throat aches with thirst, so I go over to the sink and drink till my belly sloshes around like a bucket of water. The safety drops in a tray of food—dinner—but I'm too unsettled to eat. I sit down in the chair and stare at my thumbs, which is an old habit of mine. Maybe it's an only-child thing, but when I was little, I used to make my thumbs talk to each other. I'd even draw little faces on them, some happy or surprised, silly even. But I'm too angry for that now. My thumbs would just yell and scream at each other, like my parents. I stare at my thumbs for what seems like hours and try to remember what I was like back then. But I can't. It seems like that part of me died without me even knowing it.

Finally a safety opens the door.

"Not so funny anymore, is it?" I recognize him from earlier that day, not the one who tackled me, but the one who first told me to stop. I glare at his mucky boot heels as he leads me out to the lobby, where Tracy is waiting. She crosses her arms over her chest and looks at me like I should have known better.

"I left my dinner behind. Can I go back and get it?" I ask. I'm suddenly starving. Tracy agrees, but the first-floor safety tells me dinnertime is over and besides, it's already been thrown out.

"Seems you caused quite a ruckus out there today," Tracy says to me on our way up to the third floor.

"I just went for a run."

"Well, those boys don't like to exercise much, so next time you feel like running, better clear it with someone first."

When we get to the third floor, the girls are all standing in their doorways like they're waiting for me. Or more likely, gossiping about me. I want to scream at them to stop looking at me. I feel like I'm walking up a sandy hill, trying to keep from slipping backwards. Maybe I *am* going crazy. Or maybe it was there all along, waiting for a place like Sunny Meadows to bring it out in me.

Tracy waits for me in the hallway while I go to the bathroom. On my way out, I catch my reflection in the murky mirror. With my chopped hair and crazed eyes, I get a glimpse of the woman I never want to become.

My mother.

Back in my room I lie in bed and wait for lights-out, but when it finally arrives, I can't fall asleep. My stomach's growling and my limbs are tight and tense. I get out of bed and pace the floor, trying to wear myself out so I can fall asleep and end this awful day.

"You up?"

I stop mid-stride and glance down at the air vent. Him again. My mysterious stalker, whose voice I've been searching for all day. He must have heard my footsteps.

"What do you want?"

"Meet me," he says simply.

The memory of my spectacular takedown on the lawn and subsequent time spent in isolation is still fresh, but if I have the choice between pacing the room until I fall into a restless sleep and getting off the floor . . .

"I want your key," I say, speaking directly into the vent. I want there to be no mistake about it. "The key to the stairwell. That's the only way I'm coming down."

There's a long pause, and I wonder if he's considering it, if he'd *actually* give it to me.

"Okay."

"I want it waiting for me at the top of the stairwell." I know I'm pushing my luck, but I also have nothing to lose.

"Fine."

I remember Margo's matches in my backpack. A light source. I can get the key *and* find out who he is. Mystery solved.

"See you in a minute."

I go through my ritual of sneak and stealth, sure that I'm

going to get caught, but at the same time not really caring. What more can they possibly do to me? I get out to the stairwell and close the door behind me. When I turn around, I see the key glittering like a jewel on the top step. I pick it up, fit it into the lock, and twist, engaging the deadbolt, then twist it back. I give that key a big, sloppy kiss and tuck it safely into my sock.

I could go back to my room. I have the key and that's all I need, but I want to know who he is, and I have just enough courage left to try to find out. I descend the stairs quickly, finding it easier to navigate my way in the dark this time. I creep into the darkroom.

"Marco," he says from across the room. He has ears like a dog.

"Polo," I say back. With his key in my sock, I'm suddenly in a much better mood.

"Did you find what you were looking for?" he asks.

"I did. Thank you very much."

"You're welcome. Come sit."

"In a minute." I dig in my pocket for the matches. I'll give him one more chance to confess.

"I saw them bring you in," he says. "Today on the lawn. Why were you laughing?"

So, he was there to witness my bout of temporary insanity. How many others saw me? I wasn't really paying attention to who was out there watching. He could be anyone.

"You must think I'm crazy."

"Not crazy. You looked . . . scared."

"I wasn't scared. I was just . . . surprised. I did the same thing when . . ." I'm about to say, *when I got arrested,* but he doesn't need to know all that.

"When what?"

"Nothing. Forget it."

"Come sit," he says.

"Why?"

"Because you're making me nervous."

"You can't even see me."

He groans like I'm the one being ridiculous. "I told you before I'm not going to hurt you."

"I don't sit on couches with strangers. So if you want me to sit, you'll have to tell me your name."

"My name's Adam."

Adam. I rack my brain for someone I know whose name is Adam. No one, but there's still a ton of guys I haven't met. Assuming that's even his real name. I pull the matchbook out of my pocket and silently peel off a match. I want to see him, to be able to identify him in the daytime. Or if I need to, in a police lineup.

"All right, Adam, here I come . . . Marco."

"Polo," he says, and I shuffle in that direction. My hands swim in the darkness in front of me until my shin bumps into something like a couch.

"Marco," I say again.

"Polo."

He's close now. I turn toward his voice while my hand feels for the cushion. I sit down carefully.

"Marco," I say, pressing the match head to the grit, praying it's a live one. I've got exactly one chance to get this right.

"Polo," he says, and I swipe it. The flame hisses to life, and in the orange glow I see his keys, hanging on a chain around his neck. *Real close*, he said, and he was right. I raise the flame to his face as he snuffs it out like a candle on a cake, but not before I recognize the silver chain around his neck, one I've seen in the daytime.

A.J.

Adam.

"What does the *J* stand for?" I ask.

"Junior," he says slowly. There is a note of defeat in his voice. He must have been looking for me on the first day of school. That's how he got between Brandi and me so fast. And after I asked for that map of Georgia, he knew just how to goad me into coming down here to meet him—with a key to the stairwell door. But why is he going through all this trouble?

"I thought you didn't speak."

"I don't."

"But you're talking now, to me?"

"Why are you trying to run away?"

I think back to earlier that day in the pen, when I cracked my lame jokes and he smiled. He seemed so harmless then, sweet even. And he didn't ask questions.

"It's not enough for me to sneak around the dorms at night. This place is making me crazy. Don't you want out of here too?"

"I'll be the same person out there as I am in here. So will you."

"You don't know me, A.J. So don't act like you do."

"I'd like to . . . know you."

I shake my head, trying to make sense of him. He wants to know me, but he doesn't want to reveal himself. It seems to me that he's found his own way to escape, by not speaking at all.

"You know you're doing the same thing, right? By not talking."

"I'm aiming to fix that. You're my little experiment."

"I'm flattered, but why me?"

"Because you remind me of myself when I first got here—angry, scared."

"I'm not scared."

"Maybe we could help each other."

"How?"

"We could start by being friends."

He wants me for a friend, but is he willing to tell me his

secrets? "All right, Adam Junior, let's be friends. Tell me what you did to get in here."

He draws a long, deep breath and lets it out again. "I will if you will."

This feels a lot like the game we played last night, the one where I lost. But I've already told Margo about my arrest, which means it's already out there in the atmosphere, and at least he'll be getting the true version, if it's coming from me.

"What we say in here, stays in here," I say to him.

"Agreed."

"Okay, then. You go first."

He shifts on the couch, getting comfortable or maybe just stalling. I don't mind. I'll wait.

"My father died when I was eight," he says. "It was hard. On me and my mom."

"Oh," I say, and then shut my mouth, because I know this is only the beginning.

"My mom was depressed for a long time after that. We got to be pretty poor and almost got our land taken away. Then she met this man who was . . . no good."

He stops there as though deciding whether he wants to go on.

"Whatever you tell me, I'll keep to myself."

I wait in silence, counting the seconds in the dark. At last he continues. "He beat her. When I interfered, he beat me, too."

He takes a deep breath and lets it out slowly. I can't see his face, but I can hear the pain in his voice. And the shame. I know what it's like to be ashamed of something, made worse by saying it out loud. This is the thing he doesn't want anyone to know about.

"She tried to kick him out, but he—" He pauses. "The police got involved. She got a restraining order, but it didn't end there. He threatened her on the phone and followed her—almost ran her off the road. Then one night he . . ."

"A.J., you don't have to tell me if it's too hard."

"No, it's only fair." He takes another deep breath. "He came to our house with two of his buddies—real white-trash lowlifes. They were drunk, and just from the craziness in his voice, I knew he meant trouble."

I think about my mother when she's drunk, how she becomes a completely different person. But she's never been mean. Never.

"We lived out in the country," he continues. "The police wouldn't get there in time. I told my mom to hide while I grabbed what I could find—a baseball bat. We'd gotten a dog since he left. A sweet yellow Lab named Daisy. She went after them and they . . . killed her."

"Oh my God," I say. I wish this were the end of his story, but somehow I know it's not.

"I hit his buddies hard enough to send them running,

then went to find my mom. He had her in a choke hold—what kind of man does that? I pulled him off her and just started swinging. I was fourteen then and so full of rage. I just . . . couldn't stop."

He's silent after that and though I fear his answer, it's a question I have to ask. "Did you kill him?"

When he answers, his voice is filled with sadness and remorse. "Yeah, I did."

I stay quiet, letting the weight of his confession sink in.

"We went to trial," he says. "His buddies were there as witnesses. My mom was a wreck, and I wasn't much better. The jury ruled it manslaughter. The judge wanted me in a psychiatric program. I'll be here until I'm eighteen, with probation after that."

"But wasn't it . . . self-defense?"

"No. There was a point where I could have stopped it. But if I'd let him go, he would have come back. And I might not be there." He pauses. "I already lost my father."

We're both quiet. I don't know what to say. It's such an awful, awful thing to have to go through, for him to have to live with for the rest of his life. I don't know if what he did was right or wrong, and I decide it's not my place to judge him.

"I accept it," I say, not quite sure what I mean by it, but hoping he'll understand. I reach over and find his hand in the dark. I hold on tight, and he does too.

"I was really angry when I got here," he says. "Any little thing would set me off. I got in a few fights and decided one day to just stop talking. My therapist wouldn't allow it, but everyone else got used to it. And I did too."

I think about my own anger, how it causes me to say and do things I regret later. But to shut everyone out so completely . . . he must get lonely.

"How long has it been since you've spoken to anyone other than your therapist?"

"Almost two years."

"A.J., that's a long time." Maybe that's why he asked me down here, because he has no one else to talk to. Except his therapist, but that isn't the same—talking to someone who's being paid to listen. Then I think maybe our first meeting was a test, to see if I could keep a secret.

"Sometimes I think I deserve it," he says. "The silence."

"Does your therapist think so?"

"No." He laughs. "He doesn't."

"Are you afraid of people finding out about your past?"

"Yeah. Maybe that, too."

I realize then how similar we are, because I do the same thing, by not getting close to people in the first place.

"You should talk to Victor. You guys are friends, right?"

"Now you sound like my therapist."

"Maybe he's right."

He's quiet for a moment, and I hope I haven't pushed him too hard. "It's your turn," he says at last.

I take a deep breath and remind myself that this is what it means to be a friend. To reveal things about myself to another person, even if it's uncomfortable. Even if I'm ashamed.

"I stole a car. It belonged to this guy my mom brought home. He was passed out on the floor, and the keys were on his belt. I only meant to take it for a ride . . . just to get out of our apartment for a while. But then I hit the interstate, and the thought of never having to go back there made me so happy. I could just leave everything behind. Forever."

I think about that moment, driving down the highway with the sun rising over the horizon, painting the sky with streaks of purple and orange, the most beautiful sunrise I've ever seen. The day seemed so full of promise. I had no idea where I was going, no money, no *phone*, no nothing, but I was free. I'd never have to go back to my mom and her drinking or my dad and all his disappointment in me. I could start over in a new town. Be a new person. Whoever I wanted to be.

"What happened?"

"My mom called my dad, and he called the police. They caught up with me at a gas station where I stopped to fill up. I ran from them, and they chased me through buildings and parking lots. I almost got away. But they cornered me in this alley and arrested me. I got charged with motor vehicle theft and resisting arrest. The judge gave me probation, but my dad had my probation transferred here."

"Why'd you run away?"

I think about the last year living with my mother, all the nights she went out drinking, all the mornings I had to get her up, dress her, and drive her to work, sometimes while she was still drunk from the night before. She was such a mess and it was so hard, seeing her like that, worrying she was going to crash her car and kill herself, or someone else. I should have thought ahead, gotten a job and saved some money. But I didn't want to leave her.

"My mom made me a promise." I see her face in front of me when she said it, so earnest and true, so . . . sober. "She told me she would stop drinking. For good. And she would take care of me. But she broke her promise . . . again and again."

And where is she now? Probably drinking at one of her usual dives, letting some creep with a beer gut hit on her just so she won't have to go home alone. But she was never alone. I was with her. Through it all, I was there.

I feel a flash of anger at her weakness, her *illness*. But it isn't an illness, it's a choice. Every time she puts that poison to her lips, she's choosing *it* over me.

Tears burn in my eyes, and I squeeze them shut. His arm circles around my shoulders, drawing me nearer. I press my ear to his chest, listening to the steady drumming of his heart.

I hate crying in front of people, looking weak. I hate playing the victim. *Just like my mother.*

"It's late. I should get going." I ease out of his arms and start to stand.

"Taylor, wait."

But I can't, because my head's caught up in a cloud of all the crap I'd rather leave undisturbed. I wish I could sever these feelings completely, erase all the bad memories from my mind and begin fresh. No bad dreams, no hard feelings, no anger. Just me and my happy, smiling thumbs.

I cross the room blindly, feeling my way along the hallway and onto the stairwell. I climb the stairs two at a time. Only when I'm back in my room am I able to breathe normally again.

He tries to talk to me through the vent, but I need to be alone right now. Completely alone. I stuff some dirty clothes into the vent and drop my duffel bag on top of it.

I hear Sandra's footsteps coming down the hallway.

"What's going on in here?" she asks me, hands on hips.

"Nothing."

"You are the worst sleeper I ever met." She points at my bed and waits for me to crawl up into it. After she leaves, I bury myself under the covers with the pillow over my head and Tatters against my cheek. I feel something pointy jabbing my heel.

I still have his key.

CHAPTER 8

I see him the next morning on walkover, staring at me from across the lawn like I betrayed him, and in a way, I have. I walked out on him after he shared so much of his own painful past with me. But I don't want to explain myself, and I can't tell him it won't happen again. As far as his key goes, he can always make another one.

In first period Sulli tells me the story of how I assaulted a safety, then tried to flee by climbing the fence, then had to be tackled and carried, in submission, to the first floor. The last part, at least, is true.

"Baby, you are *for real*," he says, raising one hand to fist-bump me. I stare at his tattooed knuckles, H-A-R-D. Hard what? I leave him hanging, because I'm not proud of what I did. In fact, it was pretty dumb. Now all the safeties will be watching me for the first sign of flight. Not the kind of attention I wanted.

"So, you want to go with me to the dance?" he says. "I could give you a boost over the fence."

I'm temporarily thrown by his offers—both of them. "What dance?"

"The Harvest Ball, baby. You and me. What do you say?"

In front of me Brandi stops what she's doing and listens. The last thing I need is for her to think I'm trying to make a move on her man, if they're even together.

"No thanks, Sulli. I'm not going."

He nods and smiles knowingly. "Playing hard to get, huh? I like it."

This dance business seems to be all anyone can talk about for the rest of class. Who's going with who, what the theme will be. I wouldn't think they'd have dances here at all, but I guess it's just one more way to make Sunny Meadows seem like a normal high school. More pictures for the brochure. More lies.

Later that day I stand with Margo in the pen while she lectures me on how dumb it was to try to run away in broad daylight.

"Seriously, T, I thought you were smarter than that."

"I wasn't trying to run away." At least, not on purpose.

"Well, the upside is that your popularity is off the charts. You'll have no problem getting a date to the Harvest Ball now."

I groan. The Harvest Ball again. The last thing I want is to go to a school dance, to be looked at or laughed at or gossiped about. I'm used to keeping a low profile in school—that's how I survive being the new kid all the time. I also don't feel like dressing up or acting happy. Because I hate it here. So I tell Margo the same thing I told Sulli. "I'm not going."

"T, don't be silly. Of course you're going. This is my year to be voted Autumn Queen. You don't want to miss my crowning. Victor can smuggle us in some drinks. It'll be the most, to say the least."

"I don't drink, Margo, and you can take a picture of your crowning for me."

"That hurts me, T, it really does. So who do you have in mind? For a date, I mean."

My eyes flick over to A.J. standing with Victor and another guy across the pen. Only for a second, but that's all it takes for Margo to pounce.

"I knew it," she says, and links her arm with mine. "Come on then. Let's go make all your little dreams come true."

I still feel awkward about last night. And I like him—as a friend—but I'm not about to put myself out there with all these people around. Besides, there's no telling how he might feel. "Margo, he's not interested."

"Of course he's interested. You're totally hot and you're *my* friend."

I try to physically resist her, but she's stronger than she looks. I'm so nervous about what she might say to him and how he might react that I can hardly look up, but it doesn't matter, because he and Victor are already in the middle of something, and it doesn't look good.

Margo and I stop a few feet away. The tall kid Victor's talking to has a snarly look on his face, and his movements are jerky and ragged. Victor's trying to talk him down, but the kid's only getting more and more worked up, gesturing wildly with his long, skinny arms.

"Oh no," Margo says as the kid shoves Victor back. In a flash A.J.'s there between them.

"What are you going to do about it, retard?" the kid yells at A.J. with his nose right up in his face. They're the same height, but A.J.'s got about twenty pounds on him, and I can tell he's ready, his shoulders and arms tense. A.J. stares the kid down while safeties shout from all directions, closing in fast. The kid falls back like he's going to walk away, then comes back with a fist. A.J. deflects the punch and the kid swings wildly. A.J. hooks one arm in front of him, ducks down low, and swiftly jabs the kid in the gut. One well-executed punch sends him to his knees, gasping for breath. A.J. takes a step back and examines the results. I watch his face for any sign of emotion. Nothing.

He glances up to see me watching and gives me a strange look. I don't have the chance to decipher it, because the safeties swarm him. One pushes him back while two more hook him by his upper arms. A.J. doesn't resist, just turns around and lets himself be led out of the pen.

I remember what he said last night about how he came here angry, looking for a fight. And all the violence in his past.

"What was that about?" Margo asks me. We're standing in the same spot, still linked arm in arm.

"I don't know."

The safeties raise up the other kid and drag him away. His manic energy is gone, and he looks ill and used up. He's the one who started it, but right now he sure seems like the victim. Victor rushes over to us. Nobody's dragging him anywhere, and I understand why he keeps A.J. around, for protection.

"This is not good," Victor says. "They're going to drug-test Cameron. I bet he'll say we gave him the pills."

I remember the kid's eyes, the way he moved so erratically. Of course, he was high.

"Did you?" I ask.

"No," Victor says defensively. "We're not drug dealers. Cigars, cigarettes, a little liquor here and there, but that's it. He got them from somewhere else."

"Does A.J. have anything on him?" Margo asks.

"Some money, maybe, that's about it."

What about his keys? I wonder, but I don't say it aloud.

"What will they do to him?" I ask Victor.

"He'll get sent to the first floor."

I shudder at the thought of it. "For how long?"

"Who knows?" Victor shrugs. "He'll deal. It's not his first time."

"That doesn't make it any better," I snap, irritated that he isn't more concerned.

"I've spent my time in there too," Victor says, then glances at Margo like *What's her problem?* They think I'm overreacting.

The bell rings, and the remaining safeties herd us back into the school building. I can't get the image of A.J. out of my head, the expression that crossed his face when he looked at me. Was it . . . shame?

Later that afternoon in my dorm room I move my duffel bag and unplug my clothes from the vent. I call down to him but get no response. In the middle of one of my attempts to reach him, I glance up to find Brandi standing in the middle of my room. I do the first thing I can think of—I pull a Charlotte and let out a ferocious roar, screaming so loud it hurts my own ears to hear it. Brandi curses me and rushes out of the room. Not until Tracy's standing in my doorway do I dare stop.

"What's going on?" Tracy asks.

"Brandi," I pant, "in my room."

"She stole my earrings," Brandi shouts from across the hall.

Earrings?

"What earrings?" Tracy asks.

"My *gold* hoops."

"Did you take her earrings?" Tracy asks me.

"No."

"Yes, you did too, you crazy bitch. Trish and Stacia can't find theirs, either."

I didn't take them, but I can guess who did.

Tracy stands in the hallway between us. "Can you prove she took them?"

"Search her room. I know she has them."

I tense up, worried about what Tracy might find if she searches my room—the money, A.J.'s key—but she only glances around briefly, not even bothering to look. "I don't see anything," she says.

"Then you must be as blind as you are stupid."

"Maybe so. But your smart mouth just lost you your phone privileges for the next two weeks."

"What? You can't do that."

"I just did."

"I'm talking to Kayla about this." She storms down the hall, and I nearly laugh out loud.

"Thanks, Tracy. You're awesome."

"Mm-hmm, and don't you forget it."

I try calling down to A.J. a few more times that night but get no response. I look for him the next morning on walkover, but he isn't there. In line I ask Margo if she's heard anything.

"Don't worry, T, he'll be out in time for the dance."

I clench my fists. "I don't care about that stupid dance, Margo. I don't even want to go."

"I bet you'd go with A.J."

"Ugh, you're making me crazy."

I glance up and see Brandi and her crew walk by, minus their earrings. Their earlobes look strangely naked, and they seem to have lost some of their menace as well.

"What'd you do with their earrings?" I ask her.

"I buried them someplace they'll never be found. I'm doing them a favor, really. Hoop earrings are so passé."

"You should have included me."

"Next time, T. You've gotten a lot of heat lately. You can make it up to me by coming down to my room this afternoon. We need to pick out our dresses for the Harvest Ball. It's only eight days away."

"Dresses? Where'd you get dresses from?"

"It's in the welcome packet. Everyone brings a dress, and lucky for you, I happen to have a few extra."

"Margo, I really don't want to go to this dance."

"But you will, Taylor, because you're my friend and you'd do anything to make me happy."

I shake my head at her. Not many people amuse me, and even fewer can get me to do what they want. Unbelievably, Margo can do both.

School passes by in a daze. I keep hoping to see A.J. in the hall, but he is nowhere. In the pen that day, I make a beeline for Victor. I want information.

"The safeties trashed our rooms," he says, "but they didn't find anything. We're too good for that."

"Where's A.J.?"

"Back in the dorms."

"Is he okay?"

Victor pats my shoulder. "He's fine. He likes being by himself."

No, he doesn't, I think, frustrated that I can't do anything to help him. I remember A.J.'s voice in the basement, his sad story and the loneliness that loomed so large. Then I had to go and run out on him.

The bell rings, and I continue on to automotive, where we work on the Bronco. Turns out, all it needs are some new belts, hoses, and an alternator, which have already been ordered. I watch the car keys trade hands. I'd only need the key for about a minute by myself to make a mold, assuming A.J. will help me with the rest. But what can I use in place of plaster?

Margo won't let up on me about this dance, and A.J.'s not responding to my calls through the vent. I need something to take my mind off him, so that afternoon during leisure I corner Kayla in the common room and ask if I can go down to the second floor. I need to try on some damn dresses.

"Why?" Kayla asks me suspiciously.

"Margo wants me to pick out a dress for that dance thing."

"The Harvest Ball?" she says, her voice rising an octave.

"Yeah. That."

"Of course you can. I'll take you there myself."

I follow her down to the second floor, where she hands me off to Tabitha, the second-floor intern. "You *have* to show me your dress after you pick one out," Kayla says before leaving.

Margo meets me in the hallway, wearing a black satin slip dress that cuts above the knee on the left side and drops down to the floor on the right. She's adorned it with a feather boa and a long black cigarette holder, minus the cigarette. She's even penciled in a fake mole on one cheek.

"First dress," she says. "Not my favorite, but what do you think?"

It looks great on Margo, but I want it for myself. I like its simple lines and soft sultriness. "I want that one," I say, "without all the weird stuff."

"Don't you want to see the others first?"

"No."

"So that means you're going, then?"

"I guess it does."

She smiles, and her dimple smudges her fake mole. "Come to my room and try it on. I've got a ton more dresses to show you."

Walking into Margo's room is like stepping into a backstage

dressing room. She has clothes everywhere—scarves, hats, and costume jewelry strung from every post and knob, a fluffy shag rug and lavish comforter, black-and-white posters of movie stars on the walls, and enough makeup on her desk-turned-vanity to service the entire floor. She has five opened trunks vomiting clothes and shoes—more pairs than I can possibly count. Her room looks so . . . lived in. How long has she been here to collect all this stuff?

"Wow, Margo, where's your room?"

She giggles and disappears behind a Japanese dividing screen. I glance around and notice all her packs of gum and empty containers of Tic Tacs.

"What's with all the breath fresheners?"

"I suck on them at night," she says. "It helps me fall asleep."

My eyes come to rest on an unopened pack of Bubblicious, and I get a brilliant idea. Maybe bubble gum would work as a plaster for a mold. It's soft and pliable. I glance to the screen where Margo is throwing her dress over the top, then reach over and slip the pack of gum into my pocket.

"Have at it," Margo says, reappearing in a silk kimono and holding out the black dress to me. I feel a little bad that she's invited me into her room and I swiped her gum, but she has plenty more. And knowing Margo, it probably wasn't even hers to begin with.

Behind the screen I shrug off my jeans and T-shirt and

pull the dress over my head. It falls past my shoulders in a whisper. I don't have too many curves, but the ones I have are quite apparent in this dress. And it's so light, it's like wearing nothing. I come around the screen and show her.

"T, you look gorgeous. Where have you been hiding those legs?"

I glance down. I haven't seen my own legs in a while. I need to shave, which means asking Kayla for a razor and having a safety supervise me, which is a good enough reason for me to wear pants. I glance around the room and remember that the only mirrors we have are the creepy playground mirrors, but I don't need to look. It's comfortable and practical. This is the one.

"Me next," Margo says. She hands me a couple of raffle tickets. "This might take a while. Go bother Tabitha for some sodas and make mine a diet."

Margo has soda privileges. I wonder how that's possible with all her smoking and setting things on fire, but she does seem to get her way a lot. I stop by Tabitha's room and trade the tickets for a Dr Pepper and a Diet Coke, then drag a chair from the common room out to the hallway. I finger the dress's silky material and think more and more that this dance might be the perfect opportunity to make my break. It'll be dark and loud, kids will be everywhere, the safeties will be distracted. . . .

Meanwhile Margo models her collection of evening gowns, strutting down the hallway like it's a runway. A few of the other girls pass through long enough to give us strange looks, but for the most part, they keep to themselves.

"What do you think about this one?" she asks, pivoting expertly and throwing out one hip. It's her seventh dress, a deep blue, strapless wraparound, which she's wearing with barely there silver heels.

"It's pretty. You look . . . tall."

"Do you like it more or less than the last one?"

"More. Definitely."

"The last one wasn't that hot, was it?"

"It was totally hot, but I can't even remember it now because you look so hot in this one."

"One to ten, Taylor. I need quality control."

"Nine and a half."

Margo gives me a satisfied nod, then totters back to her room to change. I pop some gum into my mouth and chew, thinking I need to know more about what goes on at these dances. Margo would be great for that, but the last time I mentioned my school project—aka escape—she got all huffy with me.

"Last one," Margo calls.

She glides down the hallway in a wine-colored Renaissance gown with a tight-fitting bodice and satin trim. It isn't the dress so much as the way Margo carries herself, head held high, shoulders back. Like a queen—regal and strong.

"That one's my favorite," I say. "I give it a ten."

She smiles. "Hair up or down?"

"Up. It shows off your neck."

"Yes, I think you're right." She twirls once, and the fabric balloons elegantly around her legs. "I'm beat. Let's take a break."

Ten minutes later we've changed back into our regular clothes and are crowded into the handicapped stall in the second-floor bathroom so that Margo can smoke a cigarette. She's got a toilet-paper tube stuffed with dryer sheets, her own invention, which she blows the smoke through to hide the smell, but the bathroom still reeks, only with a dash of spring.

She's sitting on the back of the toilet with her shoes on the seat, gazing at the murky window, when I notice she isn't sucking her cancer stick with her usual vigor.

"What's up, Margo?"

She shakes her head, and her blond hair frames her face in soft wisps, so that she suddenly looks much younger, or maybe it's because I rarely see her without her makeup on. "I'm nearing the end of my program."

"I know, Margo. You're lucky."

She sighs and takes another puff, discarding the tube and

letting the smoke escape from her nostrils like a dragon.

"I don't understand. What's the problem?"

She sits up straighter and stares at me. "You still don't know who I am, do you?"

I don't know what she means by that. I feel like I know her pretty well, even if we haven't been friends for very long.

She hops up off the toilet and does a little tap dance on the tile floor, then sings out in a child's voice, "Eat your Vitabites every day, and you'll grow up to be strong someday."

I have a flashback to when I'm eight years old, eating the marshmallows out of my Lucky Charms and watching morning cartoons when a Vitabite commercial comes on. The hair, the dimples, the demented flight attendant smile in the making. A younger version of Margo Blanchard.

"*You're* the Vitabites girl?"

"One of them. That lasted until I was ten. Then I had bit parts in a couple movies, some catalog work. Then, when I was fourteen, I just . . . fell apart. I was hospitalized for a couple months. After that I was just so tired. I wanted to sleep forever. My agent told me I'd lost my sparkle, and my parents started fighting all the time. I stopped eating or getting out of bed. That's when they decided to send me here."

"How long ago was that?"

"Two years this November," she says, holding up two slender fingers like a peace sign. "I always talk about getting out of here and moving to New York or L.A. and becoming an actor, but I don't know anything about what's going on in the world. I'm so out of touch with . . . everything."

I think about that for a moment. She and A.J. have been trapped in here for two years. It's been less than a week for me and I already feel totally disconnected from the outside world. For Margo, leaving Sunny Meadows would be like waking up from a coma.

"What if I get out and I can't handle it?" Margo says. "What if I fall apart again?"

"You'll learn fast, Margo. It's not so different from being in here."

She shoots me a doubtful look.

"For real. You're like . . . a force of nature. The first time I met you, you totally scared the crap out of me. You fight back against bullies like the Latina Queens. And you're practically running your own small business with Victor. There's so much you can do. Plus, you've got great . . ." I search my brain bank, trying to come up with what attribute Margo would appreciate the most. "Hair."

Her lips twitch like whiskers, and she almost smiles. "I'm a natural blonde, you know."

"I know," I say, and nod emphatically.

She takes one last drag from her cigarette and throws it in the toilet. It hisses back at us like a snake.

"Okay, T, I've had my confessional. Let's hear yours."

"What do you mean?"

She rolls her eyes at me. "Every time I look at you, you're staring at the fence or else scoping out the safeties. Not to mention the map of Georgia. I know you want out of here."

There's no point in trying to hide it from her; she's too observant. But if Margo knows and A.J. knows . . .

"Are you going to tell somebody?" I ask her.

"No, but you should know that Sunny Meadows has zero tolerance for runaways. You saw what they did to you just for running *inside* the fence."

"They'd have to catch me first."

Margo looks at me. "They will."

"What about the Harvest Ball?"

"What about it?"

"What's the security like?"

She shakes her head. "They've got safeties everywhere—on the lawn, in the gym, in the bathrooms. Besides, even if you got over the fence, where would you go after that? There's nothing out there but ticks and mosquitoes. And no one comes down that road unless they're coming here. They'd send out a search party and find you before morning."

"Not if I had a car."

Margo grabs me by my shoulders and gives me a light shake. "Not on the night of the Harvest Ball. They'll be expecting it, and it would really ruin my reign as queen. Everyone will be talking about you instead of me. Don't you care about my feelings at all?"

She wilts into the saddest pout I'd ever seen. Her eyes even get a little misty. What an actress.

But she may have a point. It's bad timing to try an escape when they're fully staffed. And I sure don't want to get tackled or thrown into a time-out room again. That would really ruin the ball for me, not to mention Margo's dress. I need a better plan than climbing the fence. I need a car. I think of the gum in my pocket. Maybe by then, I'll have one.

"Fine," I say at last, because she's still looking at me, waiting for an answer.

"Promise?"

"I promise I won't run away on the night of the Harvest Ball."

She hugs me tightly and it takes me by surprise, her gesture of friendship. I never really had a girlfriend before, definitely not the BFF kind, where you trade clothes and talk about boys and prison breaks. Maybe because I never felt comfortable bringing anyone home, not knowing what state our apartment or my mother would be in. I never found a girl I could trust to keep her mouth shut. But at Sunny Meadows everyone has their own baggage they're dealing with, so there isn't so much shame in it. And we're forced to be with one another all the time—part of why I hate it—but in this case, it's kind of . . . nice.

"It's time," she says, "for me to show you how much fun Sunny Meadows can be."

Twenty minutes later during "outside activities," we're flying down the hill behind the dorms on cardboard boxes Margo convinced one of the maintenance guys to pull out of the recycling bin for us. The scattered leaves help us zoom faster and soften our falls. The safeties watch us from the top of the hill with their arms crossed, but from a distance, it looks like they might be smiling.

We go up and down, over and over, headfirst and butt first. We make a train with our arms and legs, with Margo as conductor. I haven't acted like such a kid in so long, and it feels good to just let go and have fun.

A couple of more kids join in. I keep hoping to see A.J. among them, but he never appears. Margo convinces me to race some guys for Twinkies, and we wind up winning, while others compete to see who can wipe out with the most style. Sulli proves to be a real daredevil, sliding down backwards and somersaulting at the bottom.

"I think he's trying to impress you, T," Margo says with a mischievous grin.

Then kids just start tumbling down the hill, crashing into one another along the way. That's when the safeties tell us it's time to pack up and get ready for dinner. On our way up the hill, Margo throws her arm around me and belts out the most obnoxious pop song from a few years back and I sing along, if only to repair her off-key rendition.

When we finally break away to go to our separate floors, I think about how she's being released soon. It seems our friendship is destined to be short-lived. I'm really going to miss her.

CHAPTER 9

All weekend long I call down to A.J. but get no response. On Monday morning I finally see him on walkover, but he won't look at me, at anyone. His eyes are focused straight ahead, and I wonder if the first floor has done some permanent damage to him. After a couple of hours in there, I thought I was going insane.

Later that day I see him standing with Victor and some other guys in the pen, but not interacting. I wait for him to come to me, even look at me, but he won't.

"Is he going to ask you to the dance or what?" Margo says, following my gaze. I can tell that she's concerned about him too, that it's not just about the dance. "Maybe you should go talk to him, T."

"I don't think he wants to talk to me."

She nudges me a little. "Of course he does. Do you want me to come with you?"

I glance over at him, staring off at nothing. He needs a friend right now, and that's the least I can do. "No, I got it."

"Okay." She squeezes my hand. "Remember, you're prettier when you smile."

I leave Margo's side and make my way over. Halfway across the sea of asphalt he glances up to chart my progress. His face is so completely absent of emotion—I can't read him at all. I stop just in front of him, and he waits for me to speak.

"I called down to you all weekend. Did you hear me?"

He nods but says nothing. He's still not speaking. Maybe not even to me anymore.

"Did they find your keys?"

He shakes his head no.

"Was it hard?"

He shrugs. He's not going to talk to me here in the daytime with everyone watching. But maybe he will tonight, alone in the basement.

"Will you come down to the darkroom tonight?"

He looks at me with uncertainty. Maybe he's remembering how I walked out on him the last time. Suddenly I feel really bad about it, bad enough to want to explain myself.

"Listen, about what happened the other night . . ." I stare at my hands so I don't have to look at him. "You didn't do anything wrong. I just . . . I wasn't ready for . . . all that."

He grabs my fidgety fingers and does something totally unexpected—he pulls me into a big bear hug. I squeeze him back and to my surprise, it doesn't feel wrong.

"No touching," a safety barks at us, and we promptly part.

With the rush of good feelings I risk a glance up at him, which is a mistake, because he's looking at me with a little smile playing on his lips. My face burns with embarrassment, and I can't figure out why.

"W-well . . . ," I stutter, "guess I'll . . . see you later."

I turn and walk back across the pen before I can get any stupider, trying to act normal and ignore the stares that people are giving me and most likely him, too.

Margo smiles at me like a maniac and starts singing, "Taylor and A.J., sitting in the tree, K-I-S-S—"

"Shh," I hiss, but she won't, so I jab her in the ribs until she quiets.

The bell rings, and I continue on to automotive, where we're hard at work on the Bronco. I volunteer to turn the engine over. Mr. Thomas slaps the keys in my palm, and I feel my strength returning. There is nothing like the feeling of car keys in your hand.

I climb into the cab while Mr. Thomas and a few guys are still tinkering with the engine. I pull my plastic soap case out of my pocket. The soap is gone now, replaced by Margo's bubble gum that I spent all of Sunday chewing and then smoothing out on the bottom half of the container, all in preparation for this moment.

"Taylor, give it a go," Mr. Thomas calls while I'm slipping

the key off its ring. My hands are sweating so bad I nearly drop it. I shove my container between my knees and jam the key into the ignition. When I turn it, the starter whines, but the engine doesn't turn over. Mr. Thomas raises his hand to stop me.

"Give it a minute," he says.

A minute might be all I have.

I remove the key from the ignition, lick it so it won't stick, press it carefully into my gum, then lift it out again—painstakingly slowly—so that it doesn't stretch the impression left behind. I repeat the process for the other side and take a second to examine my results. I hope it's good enough.

"Taylor."

I glance up to see Mr. Thomas waiting with his hand raised. I smile as though I'm embarrassed, slip the key back onto the ring, and fit it into the ignition. I twist it, and the Bronco roars to life. The thrill that races from my head to my toes in hearing the sound of that engine is incredible. I hop out of the cab to join the guys in their celebration, receiving lots of sweaty man hugs. Then the Bronco dies, which means we're not there yet. I tap the container in my pocket like a lucky talisman.

After school I have therapy again, my second session. We meet three times a week, which is three more than I'd like. Dr. Deb starts in with more questions about my family, but

I'm only answering the questions I want to answer. It's hard to ignore her, because I know I'm being incredibly rude. But I can't handle another episode like the last time.

After a long silence on my end, the questions finally get easier—*what's my favorite time of year?* (summer), *what's my favorite color?* (green), *what do I like to do for fun?* (listen to music). Then she asks me if I've ever had a boyfriend, which could lead to something more personal, so I keep quiet and stare at the clock until my time is up.

It's the longest fifty minutes of my life.

For cleaning the common area all week, I earn media privileges and decide to utilize them that night after dinner. I ask Tracy for permission to go online while *Jeopardy!* is on, because it's her favorite show and I know she'll be distracted. I fiddle around on the computer until she's really on a roll, then pull up Google Maps to study the area surrounding Valdosta. I trace the roads from memory as best I can until I find the spot where I think Sunny Meadows must be, then zoom in until I see a photograph of the dorms staring back at me, chain-link fence and all. It's a surreal moment—to be staring at the outside of my prison while knowing I'm trapped inside.

Tracy shifts on the couch.

"You're really on your game tonight," I say to her, and she nods without breaking her concentration.

I zoom out and memorize the labyrinth of country roads

that lead back to the interstate, then delete my online history so no one will suspect anything. I tell Tracy I've got homework to do and head back to my room. There I sketch out a rough map, filling in the names and landmarks as I remember them from my ride here.

I pretend to get ready for bed, stuffing the key mold into the pocket of my pajama pants. Might as well discuss business while we're down there. I lie in bed and wait for the lights to wink out and for Sandra to come by and see that we're all tucked away for the night. The time I spend waiting for everyone else on the floor to fall asleep is torturous, especially tonight when I have a feeling like soda bubbles in my stomach. I tell myself it's because of the key mold in my pocket and not because I'm going to see A.J.

Finally the small noises of the floor fade away, and I rise from my bed to play out my slow and silent dance. I unlock the stairwell door from my side and slip through, easing it shut behind me. When I turn around, I jump back and nearly fall over.

"A.J."

He's wearing an undershirt and flannel pants. His hair is still damp from the shower, and he smells good—soapy and clean.

"Is that what you wear to bed?" he says, and it takes me a moment to connect his words with his face, because I've never actually *seen* him talk before. I glance down and see that I'm wearing pretty much the same thing. I realize the intimacy of what we're doing. Seeing each other after hours, breaking the rules to be together, even if it's only as friends.

"How'd you get out?" I ask him.

"Two keys." He pats his keys where they rest against his undershirt. It's the same place where my chest always gets so tight.

"I thought this key meant something to you," I say, holding up mine. "No wonder you gave it up so easy."

"Not that easy," he says, and smiles playfully. It's a side of him I've never seen before—a teasing, fun side. I stare at his lips, at the scar that only makes him more handsome, makes him real. He stares at me intently, and suddenly the stairwell isn't big enough for the awkward silence that follows.

"Come on," I say. "Let's go down."

In the darkroom I'm all too aware of his hand on my back as he guides me across the room, even though I know the way. When we reach the couch I freeze, not knowing how close we should be. How far could this thing go in one night, down here alone, with hours ahead of us? I sit sideways with my knees up, a slight barrier, facing him in the dark.

"Your keys," I say. "How did you keep the safeties from getting them?"

"I hid them."

"Where?"

"It's kind of a trade secret."

"You don't trust me?"

He's quiet for a moment. "I dropped them down the sink drain. I figured they might search me when they got the whole story."

"Nobody noticed?"

"My back was to the camera, and the safeties are only half watching most of the time."

"It's that easy?"

"No, but I've had practice."

"Does that happen a lot?" I ask. "The fighting?" I remember how expertly he delivered that punch, with such calm and control, almost machinelike. And his face afterward was so vacant—it's an image I'd like to forget.

"It used to happen more. That's why Victor came to me. He knew guys wouldn't mess with him if they had to go through me. I used to like it, too, made me feel like a badass. Now I just feel like a thug."

"It doesn't seem fair to you."

"I could quit."

"Why don't you?"

"There's a lot of perks to the job. And we're providing a service. It just breaks down when we don't give people what they want."

They have to say no sometimes. Would A.J. say no to me?

"How does Victor get all that stuff?"

"He's got this friend from back home. He sends us care packages. Most of the stuff is legal—candy and whatever else— but for the rest, he's good at hiding the things that need to be hidden."

"Like keys?"

He clears his throat, and I feel a new tension in the air. "Some things don't go through Victor."

However they work it out is up to them, but I figure I better get to where I'm going, which is the mold in my pocket. No sense in saving it for later.

"A.J., I wanted to see you—I mean I wanted to make sure you're okay. But there's another reason."

"I'm listening."

"I need you to make me a key."

There's a long pause, and I wonder what he's thinking. I don't want him to feel like he's being used, but he's the only one I trust to do this for me.

"A key to what?" he finally asks.

"A Ford Bronco."

"The shop car."

"One of them."

He sighs deeply and I hold my breath, waiting.

"How are you going to get past the gate?"

The gate, the guard, and the fence. Three obstacles I have yet to figure out. But I will.

"I don't know, but in the meantime, I need to be ready. I need that key."

"Can't you stay a little longer? See if this place grows on you. See if I grow on you."

I smile in the dark. I like him, I really do, but I like my freedom more, and just thinking about my next therapy session makes me feel jittery and scattered.

"I can't stay, A.J. I wish I could, for you and Margo, but I'm done here."

He's quiet for a moment. "You got it on you? The mold?"

I reach into my pocket and pull out the plastic container, find his open hand in the dark, and place it there. The springs in the couch groan as he rises, followed by a squeaking noise. One dim light flickers on above us, a naked bulb he must have loosened that first night. The light shines down on his buzzed hair and casts a shadow over his eyes. He opens the case and tilts it toward the light, studying my work.

"It looks good," he says after a minute. He sounds disappointed.

"So, you'll do it?"

He snaps the case shut and jams it deep into the pocket of his drawstring pants.

"No."

I stand up slowly, thinking maybe I misheard him, but then why is he shaking his head?

"Excuse me?"

"I'm not going to help you run away."

"Then why is *my* mold in *your* pocket?"

"I wouldn't be a friend if I let you do this."

"Then give it back." I hold out my hand. I'll take it to Victor. He's a businessman, and I've got money to spend.

"No," he says. My anger bubbles up from deep within. Like lava, it pours through me and rushes up to my skin, making my nerves sing with heat. I take a moment to choose my next words carefully.

"A.J., you're not being a friend by stealing my mold—the mold *you* taught me how to make. Just give it back and I won't bother you with it again."

"No," he repeats, like some parrot who can only say one word—*no, no, no.* I reach for his pocket, and his hand clamps down on my wrist.

"I'm sorry, Taylor."

His apology only angers me more. I jerk my hand away. "Looks like you're still a thug after all."

His eyes harden. His anger is directed at me for the first time, but I don't care. I want my mold back. "I guess that's all I'm good for," he says.

With the force of all my weight, I shove him in the chest, trying to knock him off balance. But he barely moves, just rocks on his heels and jams both his hands deep into his pockets, then stands there like a stubborn mule.

"Give it back!" I yell, not caring who hears us.

"Give it a little longer, Taylor. Just a few more weeks."

I slow my breathing and don the mask, cold and unfeeling. I stare at him in the dim lighting, ignoring his silent pleas for me to understand. He's trying to control me. Just like my father. They're both trying to trap me and make me over into something—*someone*—else, because I'm not good enough the way I am.

I catch the glint of his silver chain. His keys are important to him. The chain is thin, weak. I sigh deeply and look at him, letting him think that maybe I'm giving up. Then, when his shoulders relax, I grab for his keys with both hands and yank as hard as I can. My adrenaline fuels my strength, and the chain breaks as he stumbles back. Then I'm sprinting to the darkroom door, barreling down the basement, up the stairs, and onto the third floor. I fall through the doorway and see Charlotte farther down, standing in the middle of the hallway like she's seen a ghost. The ghost is me.

I run into my room and search A.J.'s keys frantically to see if any of them looks like a car key. None. I throw them against the air vent—metal scratching metal—and pound the bed with my fists.

I don't care if Sandra catches me. I don't care if A.J. is furious at me for stealing his keys. All I care about is getting out. And now, thanks to him, I've lost my best chance of escape.

CHAPTER 10

The next morning I pull my desk over the air vent so A.J. can't hear into my room. On walkover I don't even glance in the boys' direction. In the hall I keep my tunnel vision, heading straight to my classes without lingering. I make it all the way through lunch without seeing him.

But in the pen, Margo reminds me.

"Only five days till the dance, Taylor. Is A.J. going to ask you, or do I need to break his legs?"

I think back to last night. I doubt he'd ask me to go with him, and there's even less of a chance I'd say yes. I glance across the pen to where he's standing. He sees me and raises one hand as if signaling a truce, but I'm not giving in. I want my mold. I want that key.

"Maybe he *can't* ask you," Margo says, clearly misinterpreting our exchange. "I mean, he doesn't talk, right? Maybe *you* should ask *him.*"

"That's not my style," I tell her, because I don't want to have to explain it. "Besides, I'd rather go alone."

"You won't be alone, T, you'll be with me and Vic." She

frowns. "I really thought he was going to ask you. A.J.'s such a mystery to me. I can never decide if I like him or not."

I laugh darkly. "Me neither."

That afternoon during automotive, Dominic uncovers the problem with the Bronco. One of the spark plugs was bad. Such a simple mistake, so easily fixed. But I never get another opportunity to be alone with the keys, and besides, I don't have gum for another mold. I silently curse A.J. all throughout class. At the end of it, Dominic asks if I want to go with him to the dance. I tell him I'd love to.

In therapy later that day, I sit across from Dr. Deb and act like I can't speak. I feel her frustration with me rising, but I won't be here much longer, so why waste her time or mine?

That evening Tracy makes me move my desk away from the air vent, and when I do, I hear him playing his guitar, which is even worse than talking to him, because I love music and especially his—all the dark, haunting melodies and awkward silences. I wonder if he knows I'm listening.

As the next few days pass and I'm no closer to getting out, I feel more and more desperate and out of sorts. By the Saturday of the Harvest Ball, I'm considering something drastic.

I sit on Margo's bed and watch her go through her final stages of preparation for the dance. We've been at it since early that morning—pedicures, manicures, facials. Margo asked to borrow scissors and trimmed my hair for me. I finally shaved my legs, which took *forever*. I did it with only half a heart, not even bothering with my knees.

Margo looks stunning in her burgundy gown. Her hair is a golden crown on top of her head, and her shoulder blades look like birds' wings, ready to take flight.

"How's this color?" she asks me, puckering her lips to model a splash of crimson across her porcelain face.

"Very dramatic."

She stares at her reflection, practicing the appropriate smile for when she's crowned Autumn Queen. She's been at it all day. "Too big," she says. "Too much teeth. That one's kind of bitchy. I like it." She glances over at me. "T, you're not even wearing mascara. Get over here."

I slouch over to her vanity and she fusses over my face, bossing me around as to how to contort my eyes and mouth. I try to be a good subject, but I'm really not into this sort of thing. When she's done, she turns me toward the mirror.

"Voilà."

I stare at my reflection in the murky mirror—full, pouty lips, smoky eyes, flushed cheeks, naked throat. But it's not my face, it's *hers*. My mother. All dolled up for a night on the town, putting on a fake face to the world. The longer I look, the worse I feel, like I'm trapped in a car that's headed for a brick wall. Her face, her body, her weaknesses, her addictions . . .

"I can't do this," I say to the woman in the mirror.

I get up and walk down to the second-floor bathroom, turn the faucet on high, the hottest water I can handle, and smear it around my face. I get a puddle of liquid soap in my hands and scrub until my skin is red and raw.

"Taylor, I'm so sorry," Margo says, beside herself. "I really thought you'd like it."

I shake my head. I can't speak. The soap is making my eyes water. I'm sure of it, because seriously, this is the stupidest thing to be crying about. I grab some scratchy paper towels and dry my face. I glance down at my dress, at the huge water mark staining the front of it.

"Damn."

"Come here," Margo says, and pulls me over to the dryer. She punches the metal button and I stand under it, letting the hot air fan my face and dry her dress while I focus on the dingy puke-green tile. She comes back a minute later with some makeup remover and fixes my face while I punch the metal button again and again. The dress is dry, and when the air cuts off, I know I'm going to have to say something.

"Taylor, are you all right?"

"I just had . . . a moment where . . ." I take a deep breath and rub the knot in my chest. "I looked so much like my mother."

"Oh," she says, sounding surprised. She studies me for a

moment. "Well, few of us are blessed with flawless complexions such as yours, so if you want to go au naturel, that's fine by me."

I nod, grateful that she's not going to push me any further. "Thanks, Margo, for . . . understanding."

"You're okay, though, right? You're still coming?"

"Yeah, I'm fine."

The safety calls us to line up, and I take a couple of deep breaths and put on a happy face. Victor waves to us, and next to him Dominic waits for me. His black hair is done up with spikes, and he looks like a rock star in a black dress shirt and tie. With my matching black dress, it looks as if we planned it. Then I realize Margo probably did plan it. In any case, we look good together. And even though it's petty, a part of me wishes A.J. were here to see it.

"*Mon ange,*" Victor says, taking Margo's hand and twirling her for his benefit. He compliments her gown, her makeup, her hair. As I stand there watching the two of them, I feel a little sentimental. It must be nice to have someone who adores and accepts you, despite your imperfections.

"Hey, good-lookin'," Dominic says, and gives me a brotherly peck on the cheek. "I almost didn't recognize you. You're all babed out."

"Thanks," I say, grateful he wasn't around fifteen minutes ago when I had my little meltdown.

I reach down to lift the hem of my dress so it won't get dirty on our walk across the lawn, when I see A.J. across the lobby, staring at me without even trying to hide it. I remind myself we're at war—that he's the enemy—and shift my eyes away. I think of his keys, stashed in the secret pocket of my duffel bag, completely useless to both of us. I hope he's missing them.

"Ready?" Dominic asks, offering me his arm.

"Let's go."

We make our way along the paved pathway, passing through a tunnel of safeties. The safety who tackled me on the lawn points me out to the others like, *Watch out for that one.* Margo was right about the heightened security, but it's dark, and there are so many of us that they can't possibly keep track of everyone all the time.

Dominic chats with Margo and Victor while I scan the staff parking lot. If I could sneak away from the dance, climb into one of those SUVs, and curl up in the back hatch, maybe I can stow away when the staff leaves for the night. But I've left my money in my room. I'll have to think up a reason for a safety to take me back up.

"Taylor." Margo snaps and grabs my arm—the girl is a mind reader. She pulls me into the gym and doesn't let go until the door has been shut behind us.

I scope out the inside—safeties at every exit and more

patrolling the gym and the hallway to the bathrooms. They must have hired extra staff, because I've never seen so many of them before. The dance committee has done a nice job. There's a huge black screen with an orange light behind it, to look like a harvest moon. They've scattered fallen leaves all over the floor and used pinecones and glowing jack-o'-lanterns as table centerpieces. I've never been to a school dance before, but it's nice seeing everyone dressed up. The lights are dim and the music's loud. Dominic brings me punch and then leads me out to the dance floor. He has good rhythm, and we dance with Margo and Victor in a larger group. Before long I realize with some surprise that I'm actually having a good time.

"And now, young ladies and gentlemen," one of the teachers calls from up onstage. "I'd like to announce this year's Autumn King and Queen."

There's a digital drumroll provided by the DJ, and the woman produces a large white envelope from inside her jacket. The voting was done by secret ballot in school on Friday, and the wait has been hard on Margo. She fidgets beside me, chewing on her lip and ruining her carefully applied lipstick. I reach out and squeeze her hand.

"This year's Autumn Queen and King are . . . Ms. Margo Blanchard and Mr. Victor DeMatais."

"Oh my God!" Margo says, and throws her arms around me.

Victor takes her elbow and guides her onto the stage. He fades to the background as Margo gives the crowd her Endearing-but-Not-Overly-Joyous smile, winking at the knit of Latina Queens who glare back with pinched faces. The teacher crowns them both officiously, and they descend to the floor for a slow dance reserved for royalty. The harvest moon shines on Margo wherever she goes, and she looks just like one of those actresses in the old-timey movies. A real-life princess.

I feel a tap on my shoulder and turn to find A.J. holding out his hand to me. Is he asking me to dance? I glance around for Dominic, who is chatting with some guys from Automotive. I decide then that I'm done ignoring A.J. The silent treatment hasn't gotten me very far. I need a new tactic. Maybe he's in the mood to negotiate.

I take his hand, and he leads me to the floor. Another slow song comes on, and my palms start sweating. I've never danced with a guy like this before. His hand slides down my side, coming to rest on the slope of my hip. Every time my dress shifts, I'm made more aware of how little fabric there is between his skin and mine.

Meanwhile my other hand holds his in a death grip. If I'm cutting off his circulation, he doesn't complain. My eyes are focused on his knees, trying to anticipate his movements and not trip on my dress or his feet.

He lifts my chin and points to his eyes. *Look at me,* he says without speaking. I swallow hard and train my eyes on his, letting him me lead me across the floor. But once my nervousness fades, I force myself to focus on the only thing that matters.

"I want my mold back, A.J."

He smiles like it's funny, and it infuriates me that he's not taking this seriously. I decide to take a gamble—all or nothing.

"Meet me tonight in the basement," I say. "If I don't get my mold back tonight, then tomorrow morning, I'm throwing your keys over the fence. All of them."

His smile turns into a frown, and he shakes his head slowly, like he's disappointed. I don't like to make threats, but I don't know what else to do.

The song ends, and he spins me in a slow circle. His fingertips trail down the inside of my arm, giving me chills, and he leans in so close I can feel the heat of his breath on my neck. Just when I think he might have something to say, he lets go of my hand and walks away, heading straight for the door without looking back. There he nods at a safety, and the two of them leave the gym together.

"Are you guys together?" Dominic asks, suddenly at my side. I hadn't noticed that another song came on and all around me, people are dancing.

"No. We're just . . ." I pause. "We're not together."

Margo comes over and throws her sweaty arms around my

shoulders. "This is so amazing!" she screams into my ear. "I can't believe it. Can you believe it?"

I catch Victor's face behind her, looking rather smug, and wonder if he had anything to do with their double victory. I wouldn't put it past him to use his influence as the school's black market supplier to give Margo what she wanted.

"I never had a doubt, Margo."

"Oh my God, this is my song!" she shouts directly into my ear, and kicks off her heels. "Come on, T, dance with me."

She pulls me out to the floor and we dance together, song after song. I try to lose myself in the music, but I keep seeing A.J.'s face in my mind, that moment when he leaned in close enough to kiss me.

Suddenly the music cuts off and is replaced by a deafening shriek that seems to come from all around us. It takes me another second to realize it's the fire alarm. Water starts spraying from the ceiling, and girls are screaming, Margo among them—"My shoes! I have to find my shoes!"

I chase after her. Victor catches her by the waist, her shoes in his hand. Dominic is with him, and he puts his arm around me, guiding me to the door as people push and shove on either side. The safeties close around us like a net and funnel us out onto the lawn. We stand in the wet grass in our bare feet and ball gowns as two fire trucks barrel through the opened gate. There's no smoke or fire anywhere as far as I can tell, but rumors reach us like a game of telephone—trash fire in the bathroom, caused by one of those lit jack-o'-lanterns.

I glance sideways at Margo.

"It wasn't me," she says. "I wasn't even smoking."

I glance past the school building, past the fire trucks and police cars, to the front gate, which is still wide open. The guard is nowhere in sight. Then I look to the dorms, where A.J. must be right now. Surely they must have heard the fire trucks and the commotion on the lawn, but no one has left the building.

"What happens if there's a fire in the dorms?" I ask Margo. "How does everyone get out in time with all the locked doors?"

"The doors automatically unlock," she says, then clasps one slender hand over her mouth, perhaps guessing at my motives.

"Safety first," I say to her.

All around me, people are complaining about how their shoes, their dresses, and their night have been ruined, but mine just got exponentially better.

I know how to get out of the dorms and past the gate.

CHAPTER 11

That night I unlock the boys' stairwell door for A.J. and follow the stairs down with his keys stashed all over my body—in my pockets, my socks, my bra. I make my way over to the couch and sit down. A few minutes later, I hear him come in.

"I can smell your shampoo," he says. "Are you still wearing that dress?"

"No."

"Too bad."

My face flushes with heat. How can he be so reserved in the daylight and so open down here—like two different people?

The cushions move as he sits down beside me.

"How was the rest of the dance?" he asks.

"Fine," I say, and think back to that trash fire and all that it revealed. "It actually ended pretty spectacularly."

"You know, I would have taken you."

"You never asked me."

"You weren't speaking to me."

"Hmm . . . how frustrating is that?"

He's silent, and I figure it's because I've hurt his feelings. I didn't come here to be mean. I just want what's mine. "I want my mold back, A.J."

"Where do you plan on going when you leave here?"

"To a city." I'm not giving him any details, but I've already got it mapped out in my head. I'll drive the car to Valdosta. There I'll take a bus to Atlanta. Trey has a couple of good friends who live there. Maybe they have a couch I can sleep on until I find a job.

"City living is expensive," he says.

"I'll get a job. Or five."

"What about your parents? Won't they be worried?"

"I'll call them. Eventually."

"And your probation? What about that?"

My probation, the thorn in my side. Breaking probation is a pretty serious offense, but there must be some way around it.

"I'll figure it out."

"Sounds like you've still got some kinks to work out."

"I'm leaving, A.J., whether you help me or not. If it's not the shop car, I've got other ideas. If I have to climb the fence and hitch a ride, I'll do it. I'm not giving up."

He's quiet for a moment. Then finally he says, "I thought so. That's why I went to the trouble of having your key made."

I stop and replay his words in my head, not trusting my own hearing.

"What?"

"I made you your key."

I don't believe him, but I want to. Still, I need proof. "Show me."

I hear him stand, then the squeaking of the bulb screwing into its socket. The light flickers on, and he holds up the shining, silver key. I step closer, in a trance, until I see the Ford imprint reflecting in the light. He really did it.

"I'll give you this," he says, "but you have to do something for me first."

I have no clue what I could possibly do for him. "What is it?"

"Promise me you'll stay until December."

Is that all? I think, then realize the gravity of his request. December is a whole month away. There's no way I'm staying until then.

"Okay," I say.

"You mean it?" He studies my face closely.

"I'll stay." I make my face blank, revealing nothing. "Until December."

He hesitates, like maybe he's having second thoughts, but finally holds it out to me. I pluck it from his fingers and shove it deep into my pocket.

"Thanks." I retrieve one of his own keys and hand it over. "This one's for you."

"Where are the others?"

I collect his keys from their various hiding places while he watches with some curiosity. I unwrap the silver chain from around my ankle and drop it into his hand as well.

"Sorry for breaking your chain."

"I forgive you."

He takes a step toward me, and my breath catches in my throat. He's staring at my lips. He's going to kiss me, I think. And I realize I want him to. "Besides," he whispers, "you still need to get past the gate, don't you?"

The front gate. Of course that's why he made me the key, because he's counting on that gate to keep me here.

"Yeah," I say, giving nothing away. "There's still that."

I know then that this thing between us can't go any further. Because in a few days I'll break my promise to him. I'll be gone, and it'll only hurt him more to think that I was lying to him this entire time.

"Well . . ." I begin. I should go now, *right now*, but I can't seem to tear myself away from his eyes, making my head feel foggy and dim. I take a step backwards and stumble. I laugh a little, nervous and high-pitched. "I guess we better go," I say.

"So soon?"

"Yeah. I'm tired and . . ." I don't finish my thought, just turn and walk toward the door. Behind me he unscrews the lightbulb, then follows me out of the darkroom and up the stairs. At the stairwell landing I muster up the courage to meet his eyes again. This is probably the last time I'll see him here, in our secret place. Something needs to be said, a good-bye of sorts, but I don't know how without giving myself away.

He pulls me to him, wraps his arms around me like a warm winter coat, and kisses the part in my hair. I'm suddenly gripped with emotions that are too big for my puny little heart to handle. There in his arms I want to confess everything, that I'm leaving despite my promise to him. I want to tell him I'd like to see him again on the outside, and thank him for being my friend and helping me get out of here. But if I tell him those things, he'll know I'm a liar. He'll think I'm using him, and maybe I am.

I break away from his embrace. "Good night, A.J."

I turn away and slip silently onto the floor and into my bedroom. I crawl under the covers and relive the night in my mind. My plan is coming together now, so smoothly that it seems like it's meant to be. I couldn't have done it without him. I hope when I'm gone, he'll be able to forgive me.

CHAPTER 12

I wake up the next morning feeling more rested than I have in weeks. After "Sunday reflection," I get permission from Kayla to go down to the second floor and visit with Margo. It might be one of our last times together, and I want to say a proper good-bye.

When I come into her room, she's sitting in a chair in front of her distorted carnival mirror. I really hate those mirrors. The longer you stare at yourself in them, the more you forget what you really look like.

"I'm so old," Margo says, pulling down on the skin around her eyes.

"Margo, you're seventeen." I push some of her clothes off her bed and lie down on my stomach.

"I've been out of the biz for so long. I'm going to have to start all over—new agent, new head shots. I'm going to have to sit through casting calls and wait for hours to only say one word, just to have someone tell me that I'm too short or too tall or too fat or too skinny, too—whatever."

I want to be sympathetic, but it's hard when she's basically living my dream, to be getting out of here. I wish I had her problems.

"It's better than sitting in here," I tell her. "At least you have a chance of getting paid after all that waiting."

"But what if I'm not good enough, T? What then?"

"You could try getting a job at Burger King, like the rest of us."

She ignores my sarcasm. "My mother already has a photographer lined up for me. He's got a waiting list, he's that good. I mean, I love performing, it's just a lot of pressure."

She pulls a silver flask out of her pocket, unscrews the top, and takes a long swig—vodka; I'd know that smell anywhere.

"Did Victor give that to you?"

"Maybe."

"Listen, Margo, getting drunk isn't going to make it go away. It's just going to make you feel worse when it's over."

"I want to get drunk, Taylor. I want to start a trash fire. I want my therapist to tell my team that I need more time."

"Margo, that's crazy."

"I'm crazy."

I shake my head, frustrated with her. "No, Margo, you're not crazy. You're just . . . scared." I know the feeling. I'm scared myself, of running away, of staying here and only getting worse. I glance around her room, trying to think of something encouraging to say.

"You know that feeling," I say, "right before you go out onstage?"

"Stage fright?"

"Yeah. You're worried that you're going to go out of here and mess up your lines or trip on your high heels, but you're not. You're going to blow them away, just like you always do. You're a woman who knows what she wants, and you know how to get it. You're going to be the most, Margo, to say the least."

She studies her reflection in the dingy mirror. "Stage fright, huh?"

"And another thing: You're a hundred times prettier in real life, only you don't know it, because you've been looking in that mirror for so long. It's a lie, Margo. You're better than this place. So much better. And so much stronger."

The edges of her lips curl into a tiny smile, and I feel a little better. For her and for me, too.

"All right," she says, shaking out her long hair. "It's just stage fright. A little nervousness is good, right? It's normal."

"It's completely normal. It's to be expected."

"It's to be expected," she repeats. She flashes her I'm-Not-Scared-of-Anything smile at the mirror, and I remember the reason I came here, to tell her good-bye.

"Listen, Margo, you know that school project I've been working on?"

"Yes," she says cautiously.

"Well, it's almost finished now, and I want you to know that I've had a lot of fun hanging out and . . . getting to know you. I hope we can be friends again . . . on the outside."

She turns to me with her hands folded in her lap.

"You're really going to do it, then?"

"Yes." It's all I ever think about. I've traced my route to Valdosta more times than I can count. I've looked up bus fare to Atlanta. I already know Trey's numbers by heart. I'm ready to go.

"Taylor, you know what happens if you get caught? They give you a room on the first floor. They'll keep a safety on you all the time, even when you go to the bathroom."

"I'll take my chances."

"Is it really that bad here?" she asks. "I mean, I know the Latina Queens gave you a hard time, but they've backed off. And Victor says A.J. really likes you. I mean, he's not the most normal guy, but he is pretty hot."

I think about our moment in the darkroom last night and all the confusing feelings it brought up. I promised him I'd stay until December, but I don't think I could last that long in this place, especially not without Margo.

"I just wanted to say good-bye, and to tell you that you've been a really great friend. I don't expect you to understand."

Her mouth droops into a mopey frown as she holds her arms out to me. I go over and give her a hug.

"I just worry about you," she says.

"I'll be fine, Margo."

"If only we could trade places," she says. "I could stay here and you could go. Then we'd both be happy."

I squeeze her tightly one last time. If only we could.

I walk into school on Monday morning with an extra spring to my step.

It's a beautiful day for escaping.

In automotive I volunteer to be chief key turner, but when I climb behind the wheel, instead of using Mr. Thomas's key, I use my own copy. The Bronco starts up just fine, which means the key is good. I'm so elated by the steady thrumming of the engine I feel like I could fly. I scope out a way to get inside the garage and notice that the window on the side door is fixed with regular old glass, and could easily be broken by one of the decorative cement pavers that line the flower beds outside. Then I just have to reach in and unlock the deadbolt.

After school I walk over to the mind factory, aka healing center, ready to endure my very last fifty-minute silent strike. But when I walk into Dr. Deb's office, I see something that makes me stop short.

My parents.

The last time I saw them together was in the courtroom, and before that, I can't even recall. It seems I've interrupted something, because everyone gets quiet when they see me. My mother stands and hugs me tightly. She's worn makeup and put on perfume, but it's not strong enough to hide the smell of vodka. She's lost weight, too. She's made up of skin and bone and vodka tonics.

My father only nods at me, and I remember that last time I saw him—a couple of weeks ago when I told him I hated him. I didn't think he'd come back after that. I was wrong.

"Good afternoon, Taylor," Dr. Deb says. "I invited your parents to join us today."

"Is this my punishment for not answering your questions?"

"Taylor," my father says in a warning tone.

Dr. Deb smiles and motions to the empty seat between them. "I'd like to begin this session with a mission statement from each of you," she says, "to hear what you'd like Taylor to accomplish in her time at Sunny Meadows. But first, I'd like to hear it from you, Taylor."

"I don't even know why I'm here."

"You stole a car," my father says. "You ran away from home and resisted arrest."

"Everyone makes mistakes."

"It wasn't your first mistake."

"Let's think *forward*," Dr. Deb says brightly. "Taylor, what do you hope to gain from your experience here at Sunny Meadows? What do *you* want?"

I look at her tiredly. Do I tell her what she wants to hear—that I hope to be rehabilitated, from what I still have no idea? Or do I tell her the truth?

"I want my MP3 player back," I say to her. "I want to shave my legs without someone watching. I want to eat food I can recognize when I'm hungry, and go where I want, when I want. But most of all, I want you people to stop asking me questions and let me deal with my business in my own way."

My father frowns. My mother lifts her chin a fraction of an inch but makes no comment. She knows what it's like being trapped in these places, where you can't go anywhere without getting it cleared by five different people. I have no freedom, no control. I'm not a person to them; I'm a problem that needs fixing. And there's nothing wrong with *me*.

"As long as we're making impossible wishes," I continue, "I'd like my mom to stop drinking. Really stop drinking. I want her to stop bringing creeps home from the bar and pay her rent on time. I want my father to act like a human being again and say he's sorry for leaving us. I even want my parents to get back together, because they're worse when they're apart."

I sit back in my chair and cross my arms. I think Dr. Deb might kick me out, I even hope for it, but she only nods her head. I should have known.

"Thank you, Taylor, for being so honest and direct with your feelings. Mr. Truwell, it's your turn."

My father clears his throat and looks over at me. I avoid his eyes.

"I'd like Taylor to think before she acts and consider how her decisions affect others. I'd like her to do better in school and think about her future. I want . . ." His voice cracks, and he stops to take a breath. "I want my daughter back."

His daughter. I have no idea who he thinks that person is, only that it's not me. It hurts my feelings that I'm not enough. And if he thinks he doesn't know me anymore, it's because he never did. He's the one who's changed, not me.

"Thank you, Mr. Truwell," Dr. Deb says. "And how about you, Mrs. Truwell?"

My mother's face is a mask, much like my own. I learned it from her, after all, how to shut people out and reveal only what you choose. It's not lying, it's selective telling. It's the safest way to be. It's the *only* way to be.

"I want Taylor to be happy," she says, and I can't help but scoff at that.

"Well, I'm not happy here."

She nods. She knows what this is like, to be probed and prodded, to have to defend yourself to complete strangers. So why is she letting them do this to me?

"I'm sorry," she says stiffly, and stares at her hands, bare of any rings or bracelets, just like mine. I know who she's apologizing to. It isn't my father or Dr. Deb; it's me.

My father looks over at me. "You could have come to me," he says. "If things were bad with your mother. You didn't have to run away."

"That's why you sent me here, isn't it? Because I didn't come running to you."

"No, Taylor."

"What about when you took the house because I went with Mom?"

"Taylor," my mom says, "we couldn't have afforded that mortgage. Please, don't bring that up again."

I understand now what they're doing. Teaming up against me. They can talk about me and all *my* problems, but when we talk about their dysfunction, it's suddenly not allowed. They're hypocrites, the both of them. I turn and glare at my father. "You're not the one trapped in this place. When this is over, you get to leave and go live your life. But I'm still going to be here, caged up just like Mom."

I remember all the times we went to see her when she was in rehab, the way she looked so tired and withdrawn, trapped in some fluorescent prison, just like Sunny Meadows. And what did it ever do for her? Because here she is, still unhappy, still a drunk.

I turn to Dr. Deb. "My mother has a word for what you're doing. It's the same word she used when our power got turned off, when she got fired from a job, or when we had to move again because we got evicted. What is it, Mom?"

My mom gives me an icy stare. I know she's angry, because these are the things we don't talk about. To anyone. But I can't stand what they're doing, acting like it's my fault. All this time, *I'm* the one with the problem.

"It's bullshit."

I walk out of the office, blinded by my anger and the crushing feeling in my chest. I can barely breathe, but I force myself not to run past the safeties in the waiting room. Outside I take deep breaths, trying to get on top of it, but it's coming on too fast, forcing me under. Halfway across the lawn I drop to my knees and claw at my clothes, but I can't get any air. It's unrelenting.

A.J.'s suddenly there beside me. The worried look on his face scares me even more. I lean forward and grab hold of the grass, clawing at the dirt, trying to gather my strength, trying to breathe. My chest is so tight and I feel like I'm being squeezed right out of myself, splitting in half. I tilt forward until my forehead is just inches from the ground.

"I think I'm dying," I whisper to the grass. It must be true. This is what it feels like to die. The earth shifts beneath me as tiny bugs crawl into my head, blurring my vision. My sight blinks out as the earth opens up and I tumble, headfirst, into the darkest, deepest hole.

My eyes flash open to find A.J. above me still. I gasp for breath as he smooths back my hair and points at his face. *Look at me*, he says, and I focus on his gray eyes. Neither light nor dark, gray is always in between.

"Where am I?" I ask, taking in the white room, the bed, my school uniform, wrinkled and damp, the safety standing by the door, watching without watching.

"The first floor," the safety says. "You fainted on the lawn. The nurse gave you a sedative to help with your breathing."

I sit up and feel an echo of the terror course through me. My muscles tighten, and I rub my chest instinctively. I stop when I see A.J. watching me.

"I thought I was going to die," I say to myself, and A.J. nods gravely, like maybe he thought so too. I think back to the therapy session with my parents, walking out of the healing center, trying to make it to the dorms. And then I . . . fainted? That's never happened to me before. The feeling is getting stronger, getting worse.

"Have I been out long?"

A.J. shakes his head no. But my memory of what happened right before is so hazy, like a dream I can't seem to recall. I pinch my arm and watch a red welt bloom on my skin. A.J. watches me do it.

I swing my legs over the bed and stand up to go. The room tilts like a carnival ride, and he puts his hands on my shoulder, pushing me back down, then points one finger at me, *Wait here.* He leaves the room and comes back a minute later with my father at his side. A.J. takes up a post next to the safety, like he doesn't know whether to stay or go.

"Is Mom here?" I ask my father.

"No, she had to . . . leave."

"She had to go get a drink, you mean?"

He doesn't answer me. He doesn't need to. Instead he asks, "How are you feeling?"

"I want to go home," I say. I don't know where home is, but I want to go there, someplace safe and normal. I only know it's not here.

My dad pulls a chair over to my bed and sits down. He takes my hand in his, and it feels strange. I haven't touched him in so long.

"If I take you home with me, I'll do something to upset you. We'll get into an argument, and you will get angry and leave, and you're old enough now that I can't stop you. I don't want you at your mother's house, and I don't want you running away."

"I won't," I say, but how can I be sure?

"The time for running is over, Taylor. It's time you look inside yourself. Be the warrior I know you are."

I let go of his hand and cover my face with my arms. I feel like crying. I feel so hopeless and trapped.

"I hate it here."

"You hate it because there are rules and consequences, but you need boundaries. I had your anger when I was your age, and it took me many years to conquer it. I don't want you to make the mistakes I made."

I recall the bits of stories I've heard from my grandmother and her friends about my father as a teenager, a wild one, drinking and partying with his friends on the reservation, going out to bars in nearby cities and getting into fights, a brief time he spent in jail for it. Then he met my mother, who was visiting from Tennessee. He turned his life around for her. But he didn't know that she came with problems of her own.

"I'm not going to make your mistakes, Dad."

"What about what just happened? What if you had been driving a car? Or crossing the road? You could have been seriously hurt, Taylor."

I shake my head, because that's never happened to me before. It's this place that's making me crazy. "I skipped lunch and my blood sugar was low. That's why I fainted."

But I can see he doesn't believe me. He stands up to

go. He's going to leave me, again. "I'll be back to visit in a couple of weeks," he says. "I want to hear from Dr. Deb that you're making a real effort. She wants to help you, Taylor. We all do."

I turn away from him and stare at the wall. I know if I was on my own, I'd be fine. I could manage my episodes and I could survive, which is more than what I'm doing in here.

My father pats my shoulder and heads for the door. He motions for A.J. to join him out in the hallway. I hear my father speaking softly, and I know he's talking about me. I hate it, being treated like a patient, weak and feeble, like my mother. I'm not crazy. I know my own mind.

A.J. comes back a minute later and sits down next to me, but I have nothing to say to him. He's supposed to be on my side, not taking orders from my father. He reaches for my hand, but I pull it away.

"Go away."

He sighs but doesn't leave. I want to go right now. Get into a car and drive away, lose myself in a big city where no one knows my name and I am just another face in the crowd. There I can start over and be someone else—someone better. And all my bad memories will wash away like dirty water down the drain.

"Please, A.J., just leave me alone."

He stands and shuffles his feet a little, like he's hoping I'll change my mind, but I turn away and face the wall. Finally he leaves. I bury my face into the pillow and bite it to keep from crying. I reach into my pocket and feel the metallic smoothness of the car key.

I'm leaving tonight.

CHAPTER 13

After lights-out I wait an extra-long time for everyone on the third floor to fall asleep. I linger over the air vent, thinking to call out to A.J. and tell him good-bye. But he'd be mad at me for breaking my promise to him, and he might try to convince me to stay. It's not the perfect solution, but what other choice do I have?

I stuff my pockets with the essentials—cash, keys, map, bus schedule, phone numbers, and Tatters. I sit on the edge of my bed, listening for the sounds of Sandra finishing up her rounds, then slip like a shadow down the hall. I unlock the stairwell door and follow the stairs all the way down to the basement. At the end of the hallway I find the fire alarm and rest my fingers lightly on top of it, praying that when I pull it, the door will unlock just as Margo said it would. If everyone's asleep, I'll have that much more time to get away. Every second is precious.

I take a deep breath and yank it down.

The fire alarm wails, and I push open the basement door to the cool evening air. I take in a huge gulp of it and sprint down the hill, away from the dorms, risking a glance back to see the first safeties coming out with residents trailing dully behind them. I tear across the field, staying in the shadows of the high school. Outside the garage, I grab a brick off the ground and hope the fire alarm is loud enough to mask the sound of breaking glass. I bash in the side window, taking care not to cut myself on the jagged glass, then reach through and unlatch the deadbolt from the inside.

Inside the garage, I punch the button to open the garage door, hop into the Bronco, and jam the key into the ignition. The car rumbles to life, and I swiftly back down the driveway with the headlights off, turn, and follow the maintenance road to where the front gate stands wide open, just as it was on the night of the Harvest Ball. Kids are still shuffling out of the dorms like zombies. The floor safeties have their hands full. No one's even looking my way.

The fire trucks scream toward me, but I ease down on the accelerator anyway. The first truck races past, and I brake hard. The second one follows right behind it, and as soon as it's through, I hit the gas.

I'm through the gate and down the driveway when I instinctively brake at the stop sign and look both ways. That's when a Jeep screeches to a stop in front of me. I make eye contact with the driver, a safety—a whole Jeep full of safeties. My heart beats double time as I fight the panic rising in me. Where did they even come from?

I back up and make a swift turn, racing the other away. The Jeep growls behind me, right on my tail, while the safeties shout at me to stop. I'm running blind now. I never mapped this way out. The pavement ends and I follow a dirt road, turning randomly, trying to put space between me and them, swerving and kicking up sand, praying that one of these roads leads to someplace good.

My front tires hit water, and I skid to a stop. I've dead-ended at a lake.

I'm caught in their headlights as they jump out of the Jeep and shout orders to secure me, but I'm not stopping. I'll run to the road and hitch a ride. I'll run all night if I have to. I fall out of the Bronco and sprint away, batting branches and hurdling over fallen trees. Thorns scratch at my face and arms, but I hardly feel them. I have to get away. They crash through the forest behind me, their flashlights throwing beams of light on the trees as they shout directions to one another, hunting me.

I come up to a chain-link fence and stop short. On the other side I see the dorm and the residents on the lawn. Terror washes over me. They've backed me up against Sunny Meadows. I turn back, thinking to lose myself in the woods, but the safeties are already there. They have me cornered.

"Nice and easy there, sweetheart," one of them says while I crouch in wait for them to advance. He takes a step toward me, and I dash through the widest space between them. But one of them catches my arm and yanks me back. I fall hard on my side. I try to stand, but he rolls over on top of me, shoving my nose into the wet leaves and dirt. They lift me by my arms as I kick the air, trying to make contact. They drag me screaming to the Jeep and drop me on my tailbone. A jolt of pain travels up my spine and makes my head throb. Two of them grip my arms on either side while another crouches in front of me and holds my ankles. A single thought cycles through my terror and fury: *How did they find me so fast?*

They drive back to the dorms and park on the lawn, where everyone is watching, wide awake. They haul me out of the Jeep. My eyes fall on A.J. standing beside a safety, looking terrified and sick to his stomach.

I see the guilt in his eyes, and that's when I know. He told them. That's how they found me so fast. He must have been listening to me pack up through the vent. Or maybe he was down in the basement while I was leaving. He knew every move I was going to make. That's why he gave me the key, so that he'd know how to catch me.

It was all a trap.

My anger hits like a wrecking ball, and I start screaming at him, "You don't speak! You don't speak!" over and over again.

He begs me with his eyes, but he is false. He was never my friend. He's a spy, a fake, a phony, and I hate him for it. All my planning and preparation is for nothing. I am a prisoner. Trapped. Because of him.

"He made me the key!" I yell at the safeties, at everyone. They look at me like I've lost my mind, and maybe I have, but I want everyone to know. He gave me something to stand on, then ripped it away to watch me fall.

"He has all the keys," I scream, "to all the locked doors! He goes wherever he wants!"

My thoughts dissolve into garbled nonsense as they carry me through the lobby and onto the first floor. They drop me in a time-out room and shut the door behind me.

I collapse on the ground with my cheek to the cold, hard floor and howl.

CHAPTER 14

They move a bed into the time-out room. The cardboard trays come three times the next day, but I don't care enough to eat. The fluorescent light goes out at night and flickers on the next morning. The window changes colors. There's a camera behind a cage that watches me like an insect eye. There is no escaping it.

Dr. Deb visits. She wants to talk, but I start laughing and can't stop. After she leaves, another woman comes in. She says her name is Pamela and she'll be my personal safety. I recognize her from my first day here, the one who checked my head for nits. She looks as though she hasn't smiled in twenty years.

Pamela leads me to a room farther down the hall where there is a bathroom and a shower, tells me to undress, then watches me do it. She turns on the water, and the shower spray feels like a million tiny spears piercing my skin. Pamela hands me a bar of soap and tells me to wash myself. When I'm done, she shuts off the water and hands me a towel and a stack of clean clothes. My underwear is baggy and hangs off my hips. I haven't been eating much.

Back in the room I sit on the floor and count the flecks on the linoleum. There are proportionately fewer dark brown than light brown, and even fewer greens. I search for shapes in them, like I might with clouds. I time the heater to predict when it will shut off and come back on. My eyes flash over the air vent a hundred times an hour.

I hate him.

The light goes off again. Nighttime. I lie in the bed and drift in and out of consciousness. I dream of my grand-mother's hands, her fingernails hard and smooth as river rocks, caked with dirt from working in the garden. I dream of her eyes, shining in the lamplight of the evening as she sat with her head bowed over her sewing machine, patching together skirts with patterns more brilliant than daylight. I dream of her storyteller voice. . . .

"Time to get up."

The light flickers on, and Pamela is there instead. I want to dream longer. I want to never wake up. I close my eyes and try to find my grandmother, but she's gone.

"You're off observation," Pamela says flatly, and strips away the thin blanket, exposing me to the cold air. "Follow me to your new room."

She opens the door, and I walk out to the hallway. A hope-ful feeling rises in my chest, but she stops before we get off the floor. It's a door just like the other one. It seems I'm living in a nightmare, because I can't stop the door from opening or prevent my feet from moving forward. There is the same white bed, same metal chair. The only difference is instead of a camera there is a metal rack across the back wall where my school uniforms hang. She tells me to put one on; I must go to school.

I'm suddenly immobilized by fear. The stares and whispers behind my back, I don't have the strength to face them. And A.J. I don't want to feel the anger and betrayal. I don't want to feel anything, ever again.

"I don't feel well," I say to Pamela.

"The nurse has cleared you for school."

I stare at my uniform. The thought of having to put it on makes me want to tear my hair out.

"It will be easier if you dress yourself," Pamela says, letting her threat hang over me like a noose. I put on my clothes. I have no other choice.

Pamela shepherds me across the lawn, and I watch my feet shuffle over the dead grass. The sky is bleached of its color, like a sheet that's been left on the line too long. Inside the building it's stuffy and crowded. The desk confines me, and I can't get a full breath. Brandi stares at me in shocked silence as I claw at my clothes. Sulli helps me out to the hallway, where Pamela is waiting.

I sit on the floor and stare at the industrial carpet, at all the different hues interwoven to form the resulting color, which is an ugly, nothing blue. Finally the feeling passes.

"Back to class," Pamela says, showing no mercy.

In the pen Margo comes over and tries to talk to me, but Pamela won't allow it. "No socializing outside of class or group," she barks. Pamela is a Doberman with big, lethal teeth.

Margo retreats to Victor, and they bob like buoys on the water. There is an ocean between us, and I don't have the will to bridge it. A.J. is there too. He stares at me from across the pen like he's in pain. I avert my eyes. I hate him more for his apologetic looks.

Automotive therapy has been replaced by independent study. In class I don't lift my pen and I don't raise my hand. I just don't care. I stare at the grain on the laminated desks and imagine I'm in a deep, dark tunnel underground.

Days drift by like clouds.

Margo gets bolder in her attempts to reach me. She rushes up to me in the hallway, squeezing me so tight it hurts my ribs. I can smell the smoke on her clothes and her perfumey hair. A rush of memories flood me and for a second, I feel the embers of my former self ignite.

"No touching," Pamela snarls.

"I love you, T," she whispers. She walks backwards, away from me.

The next day Sulli tells me in first period that Margo's been released. That night, alone again in my room, I lay my head on my pillow and try to feel sad about Margo's release, but I can't, and it frightens me.

I meet with Dr. Deb for therapy three times a week. I don't have the energy or desire to speak, so I stare at the window until the sunlight makes my eyes burn. She says this program isn't working, and she's going to talk to my team about having my privileges reinstated. I have no opinion on the matter.

Another week passes. It's December now, and the trees are dropping their leaves like tears. I stare at their skeletal frames and think they must be the only ones who know how I feel. Pamela loosens my chain. My classmates are now allowed to speak to me, and some of them do, but I have nothing to say back.

Pamela makes me attend group activities, but she can't force me to participate. I pretend I'm a lizard and time how long I can stay absolutely still without blinking.

One day in assembly, A.J. finds me and sits down next to me. I know it's him without even looking over. He's been waiting for this opportunity, when I'm a captive and can't simply walk away. What more could he possibly want from me? I wish he'd just leave me alone.

"Taylor," he says. The pulse of my name on his lips is so familiar I can hardly bear to hear it.

"You don't speak," I say to him, though I know it's not true anymore. I see him sometimes talking to Victor and the other guys. Selfishly, I wish that he didn't speak, because that would make it easier for me to ignore him.

"I want you to know how sorry I am. I should have never—"

An icy pain rakes across my chest. I stand up and walk away as fast as I can, sucking in ragged breaths, trying to keep it together. Pamela follows me outside and snaps at me to "*get back in there.*" She won't let me sit anywhere else, so I take my seat next to him and focus on Charlotte in the row in front of me. I stare at her curly red hair and imagine we are mermaids swimming free in the ocean.

Over the next couple of weeks, my silence hardens around me like a mud wall. People give up trying to talk to me, even look at me. Except A.J. I avoid him at every turn, but I cannot cut off my ears.

It's a cold night, and we're sitting outside around a fire. My fingers, hands, arms are numb, but I won't put on my jacket. Because there are some things Pamela can't make me do. I clench my teeth to keep them from chattering and stare at the flames, flickering like hands, so warm and inviting.

That's when I hear it—the haunting melody of his guitar. I look up to see him staring back at me, playing this song for me. I'm so angry at him that I stand and scream at him like a madwoman. There's no order to my rant, no words, only the sheer force of my pure, bottomless fury.

His eyes are full of misery and pain, but he won't stop playing. I cover my ears with both hands, howl, and kick dirt in his face as Pamela drags me away from the fire.

I feel my wall crumbling all around me.

December brings with it Victor's release, which means the end of cigarettes and Twinkies. It's the end of Dominic's program as well. We haven't spoken since I tried to run away, but I remember the story he told me about how when he got out, he hoped to make things right at home. On his last day at Sunny Meadows, I catch his eye in the hallway. He nods as if he understands.

Winter break arrives, and most of the residents leave to visit with their families for the holidays, except for those of us who are here as part of a court order. The dozen of us leftovers are rounded up on the lawn and given jobs to do around the campus under the supervision of the mainte-nance crew and a few safeties. Pamela is just another safety now, but I remain on the first floor.

We rake and bag leaves and haul them up or down the hill. They keep us busy enough to not start trouble. It's hard work, but the fresh air helps me breathe deeply, and the long hours of manual labor allow me to sleep better at night. After a couple of days I even feel my appetite returning.

Sulli calls us the Chain Gang and makes up mildly inappropriate songs that they sing together while working. I don't sing, but I enjoy watching the safeties squirm. I'm sure they'd like to make a rule against it. We get our digs where we can.

Brandi and I are the only girls on the Chain Gang, and over the course of a week we're paired up frequently. Stacia and Trish were released around the same time as Margo, so she seems to be going through a similar kind of heartbreak. With their numbers dwindling, they no longer call themselves the Latina Queens.

"You want some good advice, Taylor?"

We're painting garbage cans when Brandi says this to me. I stop midstroke and look at her. The paint drips off my brush, two gray splatters on the dead ground.

"Play their game," she says. "You tried running away, which was a massive failure. So what are you trying to prove now? Just how crazy you are? Congratulations, you've done it. Why don't you try acting normal for a while? Answer their questions and make them think they're winning. Unless you want to be here until you're eighteen."

I continue painting, one stroke up, one stroke down, no drips, but her words have a way of worming themselves into my brain, the chorus playing over and over . . . *until you're eighteen.* Can they really keep me here that long? Maybe. It seems they can do whatever they want.

After that day Brandi and I forge an uneasy truce. We never mention what happened between us. We don't apologize and we don't look back. We're the same in that way.

A.J. is there too, always watching. I feel his presence like a safety. He's waiting for something, maybe for me to acknowledge he exists. But he may as well be a pile of leaves or a garbage can, for all the effect he has on me.

One day we're outside chipping paint on the maintenance shed when he drops a folded-up piece of paper at my feet. I stare at it among the paint flakes and wait for him to pick it up again.

"It's a note from Margo," he says. "I've been holding on to it for you."

I look at him suspiciously. Exasperation crosses his face. "Just take it," he says.

I reach down slowly and tuck it into my shoe, afraid that a safety might try to take it away from me. There are so many things they won't let me do now, so many privileges I never thought could be lost.

We continue scraping, and the tension between us crackles like a live wire. His pitying looks and his apologies didn't work on me, but his frustration I recognize—I have a few unresolved feelings myself. I tell myself he's not worth it. He's someone I thought I knew.

Later that night in my room I unfold the note from Margo carefully.

> Dear Taylor,
>
> I'm being released tomorrow, and my biggest regret is that I can't give you a proper good-bye. I wish I could stay and be the friend to you that you've been to me. We have so many things to talk about.
>
> You're a fighter, Taylor, so fight. Do what it takes to get out the hard way. Then come visit me and we'll celebrate our rehabilitation together.
>
> Remember you are strong and this is temporary. A.J. has my numbers. Call me as soon as you can. I'll see you again on the outside.
>
> With love, your friend,
> Margo

I caress the paper like it's made of silk and read it again and again. *Do what it takes to get out the hard way.* It seems she and Brandi are telling me the same thing. What if I put on a happy face and answer their questions? Every one of them. Is that all it will take to convince them that I'm rehabilitated? Could it really be that simple?

I'm still pondering it the next day when my father comes to visit for Christmas. Not my mom, though. She's never been one for the holidays. That was always me and my dad. She calls me in the morning, but I don't have much to say to her. It's not a very merry Christmas.

My dad and I eat lunch together in the dining room, which has been laid out with tablecloths and real silverware and plates. The safeties stand by like distant relatives. The only thing they're missing is the bad holiday sweaters. My father tries to engage me, but I'm less interested in small talk than ever before. By the time dessert comes I've zoned out completely, watching the whipped cream melt down the sides of my pumpkin pie.

"Taylor," my father says, "this isn't the solution."

I glance up and see the concern in his eyes. I know that my distance is scaring him. It's scaring me, too, but I don't know what to do about it.

"You're still running away," he says. He places one finger to my temple. "Up here. You're giving up. You're surrendering."

When we could not fight, we ran. When we could not run, we hid. But we never surrendered. . . .

He doesn't say the next words, but I know what they are. *Just like your mother.* I stare at my plate and think he's right. I am just like her—giving up at every turn, feeling sorry for myself, playing the victim. I hate myself for it, but I don't know how else to be.

"Try," he says, and reaches for my hand. And I know I have no other options. I have to let them think they're winning. That's the only way I'm going to get out of here. The math is simple enough. Six months or eighteen months? Until I'm seventeen or until I'm eighteen? I inch my hand toward his, and he curls his fingers around mine.

"Okay, Dad. I'll try."

CHAPTER 15

When winter break is over, they move me again. To the second floor this time. Tabitha is my new intern. She smiles nervously when she first sees me and the fake me smiles back. Rhonda, their floor safety, doesn't seem the least bit pleased about my arrival. "You cause us any trouble and it's back to the first floor."

I unpack my stuff for the first time. On the third floor, I'd kept everything in my duffel bags, but here I decide it will look better if my clothes are in drawers. It's not a surrender; it's a strategic maneuver.

On our first day back to school I stand outside the building and give myself a pep talk. I'm going to raise my hand in class and do my assignments. Like Kayla once said, *Participation is the first step to rehabilitation.* I'm going to smile at my teachers and my classmates, because I'm normal and happy. I'm going to do these things because *I want out.*

In first period Mr. Chris passes out worksheets but skips my desk, since I haven't touched anything paperish in a couple of months. I raise my hand, and it takes him a moment to realize I'm waiting for him to call on me. Finally he does.

"Yes, Taylor?"

"I'd like a worksheet, please."

His brow crinkles and he glances at the safety, who only shrugs. If we're not misbehaving, the safeties couldn't care less.

"I'd rather not waste the paper," he says. "If you don't intend to do it."

"I do."

Mr. Chris hands me a worksheet and then watches me as I uncap my pen and answer the questions. When I'm finished, I turn it in, but instead of adding it in with the others, he studies it for a moment.

"Speak with me after class."

The bell rings, and everyone else files out. I stand by my desk and try to quell the nervousness in my gut, hoping he doesn't see right through me.

"Do you hope to pass this class?" he asks.

The real me doesn't care, since I'm headed for a GED anyway, but no teacher wants to hear that.

"Yes, Mr. Chris, I do."

He crosses his arms, and I can tell by his face that it's going to take more convincing. "I don't think you've completed an assignment since you've been here."

I think back and realize he's right, but I knew what they were. I mean, I listened to everything he said. I read over the questions even if I didn't answer them. Then I understand what he's getting at—all that missed work.

"I could make up the assignments."

He sighs and shakes his head, but he doesn't say no. I have to try harder, to show him I'll follow through. "I have independent study after lunch. I could start today, working backwards maybe."

I think about how that would work, to do the assignments backwards, figuring out how it all came to be.

"I just don't know, Taylor."

He's still holding out on me. Why? I rack my brain, trying to figure out what he wants. An apology, maybe. I hate apologizing, but it's just two words, and that's a small price to pay for my freedom.

"I'm sorry," I say, but not very loud.

"Excuse me?" he says, even though I'm pretty sure he heard me.

"I said, I'm sorry for . . . having a bad attitude." That's pretty standard. I've been hearing that most of my life. And it's something I should be sorry for. Mr. Chris just wants to teach me history and he's given me a hard time, but it wasn't personal. It's not like he *betrayed* me. Not like some people.

Mr. Chris sighs. "You have been difficult."

I nod my head in agreement. "Yes, I have."

"This is going to be a lot of extra work for me. Having to go back and make an individualized learning plan."

"Maybe I could . . ." I glance around the classroom, trying to see if there's something I could do to help him out. Sharpen pencils? Grade papers? I doubt he'd trust me with either of those tasks. Then I see the huge stacks of books he has in the back of the room. Maintenance has a ton of scrap wood. And I know how to hammer in a nail. Maybe with supervision I could build him a bookshelf. It might not be that pretty, but it's better than having his books get trampled on.

"I could build you a bookshelf," I say. "And organize your books. Alphabetically or . . . whatever."

He purses his lips and glances at his small collection. Finally he nods. "We'll give it a try. I'll have your first set of assignments ready for you tomorrow. A bookshelf sounds nice too. Ms. Suzanne in wood shop could help you with that."

"Great," I say, and smile. It's progress.

In my next couple of classes, I follow the same strategy. I participate. And after class, I ask my teachers if I can make up my work. My English teacher is pretty forgiving and just asks that I read the books and answer the study questions, which won't take me too long, but my chemistry teacher wants me to retake all the tests, and my Algebra II teacher wants me to start on Unit 1 in the textbook and work my way through it, doing *all* the homework. I don't know if there's enough time in the day to do all these problems, but I have to try. I want my team to talk about what a turnaround I've made. I'm on the road to rehabilitation.

In the pen that day, I bring my math book outside with me. Instead of staring at the asphalt or counting the diamonds in the fence, I start plugging away at math problems. After a few minutes Sulli and Brandi stop by, throwing their twin shadows across my page. They're officially a couple. I suspect they always were, but now there's a lot less fighting and a lot more making up and making out.

"Whatcha up to, T-scream?" Sulli asks me. T-scream is the name he gave me on the Chain Gang, on account of my spontaneous outbursts. If anyone else called me that, I'd mind it, but Sulli gets away with it. Because he's funny and you can't laugh at everyone else without getting a name of your own.

"Math."

"Why?"

"So I can pass the eleventh grade."

"Is that what we're supposed to be doing here?" he says, always the clown.

"She's playing the game," Brandi says. "Right, Taylor?"

"Something like that."

"It wouldn't hurt for you to be seen with friends some-times," she says. "Laughing and joking around. It would make you look less like a murderer-in-the-making."

I give her my cheesiest, fakest laugh.

"Gosh, you seem almost nice now," she says with a smirk. Out of the corner of my eye I catch A.J. watching us, and I drop the act. I don't want him to think I might be looking for a friend.

For the rest of the day I continue with my *new* school project, which is getting out the hard way. But the real test comes that afternoon, when I walk into the mind factory. Everything I've done up until this point has been a warm-up. Because if there's anyone I have to convince of my new attitude, it's Dr. Deb.

"Good afternoon, Taylor," she says.

"Afternoon," I say brightly. She tilts her head and narrows her eyes. The game has changed again, and she's thinking of her next move.

"You look . . . well rested."

"I am."

"How was your vacation?"

The real me would say that a *vacation* is two weeks at the beach, not shut up in Sunny Meadows painting garbage cans and chipping paint. But the fake me smiles pleasantly enough and says, "Just fine."

"That's wonderful to hear. Did you see your father over the break?"

"Yes, we had lunch together on Christmas."

"And how was that?"

It was . . . tolerable? No, something better than that.

"It was splendid."

"*Splendid?* Well, that is good news. And what about your mother? Did you see her?"

"No," I say. I spoke with her again the day after New Year's, because that's how long it takes her to recover from a bringing-in-the-new-year hangover. I wonder if she made any resolutions. Probably not.

"She said she's going to come visit as soon as she can get some time off," I tell Dr. Deb, which is what my mom told me, though I know better than to hold her to it.

"Good," Dr. Deb says.

I nod enthusiastically. I could do this all day. Happy, happy Taylor Truwell, the big small-talker.

"And how's school going?"

"Great," I say. At least I don't have to lie about this one. "I'm catching up in my classes."

"That's a step in the right direction."

"It sure is." I don't care what direction I'm headed, as long as it's out of here.

"And how's your breathing been?"

My . . . *breathing*?

"Fine?"

"Because I've noticed that sometimes you have difficulty with that. Breathing."

She's talking about the feeling. Sneaky, Dr. Deb. She must think I'm new at this game.

"It's just my asthma," I say, knowing full well that it isn't. I shouldn't even be lying about it, but I can't help it. Even though I hate it, the feeling is still mine.

"I didn't see asthma listed on your medical record."

"Acute asthma," I say. I have no idea what that means, but I think I've heard of it before, and maybe I have it.

"Interesting," she says, which is what people say when they don't believe or agree with you. "Well, for now, let's not try and define it. Let's just focus on your breath, shall we?"

My good mood is fading fast, but I can't give up so easily. I'm going to play her game, and I'm going to win.

"Great. Let's do it."

"All right then. We'll begin by closing our eyes."

I close one eye. *Never take your eyes off your assailant.*

"Take a long, deep breath in," she says. "Visualize the air entering in through your nose, expanding your diaphragm and rib cage, filling up your lungs from top to bottom."

She models the breathing, and I follow along. One long, deep breath in and out.

"Now imagine the oxygen flowing through your arteries and capillaries, reaching the very tips of your fingers and toes. Wiggle them a little to see how the oxygen gives you energy and strength. . . . Good, now let it go. Breathe in deeply again and hold on to your breath for as long as it's comfortable. But when you release it, do it slowly, counting in your head as you exhale."

I exhale slowly, *ten, nine, eight . . .* counting backwards without meaning to, but it feels better than counting up, because at *one* it will be over, right?

"Excellent," she says. "Let's do it again."

We go through the whole sequence four or five times, then she starts coaching me as I breathe, saying, "I am powerful. I am strong. I am in control."

I have no idea what she's talking about.

"Say it with me," she says. "Between breaths. One statement at a time."

The real me doesn't believe in this corny feel-good crap, but the fake me says the words aloud. "I am powerful." I breathe. "I am strong." Breathe. "I am in control."

"How do you feel now?" she says.

"Decent," I say. "I mean . . . great."

"I'm giving you a homework assignment. Tonight before you go to bed, I want you to sit in a quiet place and do this exercise by yourself, repeating the mantra in your head: 'I am powerful. I am strong. I am in control.' Will you do that for me?"

"Sure," I say, knowing full well I won't.

But later that night I remember Dr. Deb's homework assignment and decide to give it a try. I sit on the edge of my bed and breathe in and out, but I don't think I'm doing it right, and when I say the words, they just sound silly and stupid.

I can fake it to Dr. Deb, but I don't have to fake it to myself.

"I'd like to know more about my program."

It's the following week in therapy. I'm on a reconnaissance mission to figure out the rehabilitative team's rules of engagement. Only I can't let Dr. Deb know it.

"What would you like to know?" she asks.

When does it end? I think. I want to mark my release date on a calendar and count down the days with big red Xs. But I can't say that to her. I have to be smart.

"Well, my probation is six months, so . . ." I trail off, but she doesn't fill in the blanks. I continue, "And I've been here nearly three months already, which means I must be about halfway through. I just want to make sure we have enough time to complete it—my program, that is."

She tilts her head and studies me. "We don't put time

limits on our residents' therapeutic programs. Six months is just a guideline, as I told your father already. We'll have plenty of time to complete your program."

This is crap, I think, and catch myself before I say it aloud. "That's great," I say. "I wouldn't want to rush it."

"Neither would I," she says with a smile. "Now, if you're ready, I'd like to play a game with you. It's called Yes or No."

Before I can respond, she gets up and moves to stand across the room.

"Is this comfortable?" she says.

"Yes?"

She takes a step closer. "Is this comfortable?"

"Yes."

She continues asking me and I continue to say yes, until she's standing just in front of me, so close I can see the pattern of the threads in her linen pants.

"Is this comfortable?" she says.

"No."

She backs away, and the game begins again. I respond, *Yes. Yes. Yes. No.*

We play the game in a variety of ways, with me standing, sitting, and lying down. With her behind me and to my side, in front of me and above me. At the end of the session she tells me she'd like to play the same game next week with someone else.

"Who?" I ask her.

"Who would you feel most comfortable with?"

I think of Margo and how much fun we could have with this one, re-enacting it later on. I miss her so much sometimes—her little quirks and her sense of humor, her enthusiasm.

"Charlotte," I say to Dr. Deb, and I'm not sure why. I haven't said much to her lately, but I remember how we first met. Charlotte is someone who respects boundaries.

The following week Charlotte and I play the game together, taking turns at being the one to say yes or no. When I'm able to move, I actually have less power. I'm also nervous about invading her space, but Charlotte never raises her voice against me, not like before. She seems calmer now. Maybe she's actually getting better in this place, or maybe it's me who's gotten worse.

That same week in school, Charlotte stops me in the hallway.

"Here," she says nervously, and pushes something at me. "This is for you."

I glance down at what she's given me—a coloring book, My Little Pony.

"These too," she says, and hands me a pack of twistable crayons, like the kind Margo gave her my first day here. "These are the good kind."

"Okay," I say. "Thanks, Charlotte."

"Sure," she says, then gives me a tiny smile and hurries away.

That afternoon, after I've done so many math problems I think my head might explode, I get stuck on Unit 3: Word Problems. I can't figure them out—any of them—and the more time I spend on them, the more I come to realize that I will never be able to catch up on all this schoolwork. And even if I completed every math problem, aced every chemistry test, and answered all of Dr. Deb's questions, there's no guarantee that even that would be enough. What if it's all for nothing? My release date isn't three months from now or even six months from now; it's seventeen months from now, the day I turn eighteen. I'll be in here as long as Margo. Even A.J. will be released before me.

I scold myself for even thinking about him. I set my algebra book aside and dig around in my backpack for more scratch paper. My fingers grab hold of the coloring book Charlotte gave me, and I pull it out. When I open it to the first page, I find she's already colored it in—a purple Pegasus. But even better than that is her message to me in the corner:

To: Taylor
From: Charlotte

My heart expands just a bit.

I browse through the pinups of coquettish ponies until I find one who looks just a little bit defiant. I color her red with a fiery orange mane. I draw in a devilish smirk on her muzzle. By the time I'm done with her, she's a warrior pony.

And I feel better.

I go back to my word problems and tell myself that I'm going to kill them. A couple of hours later I've completed every one. I turn the page and go on to Unit 4.

February brings with it a kind of cold I've never experienced before. An actual winter. Where I'm from we have cold spells where people turn on their heat because it's there, but the afternoons are usually warm still. Here there are stretches of days with freezing temperatures. No snow, though, just an icy cold drizzle, like there's a huge snow cone in the sky dripping down on our heads.

The girls on the second floor are crabbier than usual too. When they're not whining and complaining about one another, they're fighting over what programs to watch in the common room. I've got schoolwork to keep me busy, but I find myself longing for the days of the Chain Gang, working outdoors and feeling my muscles in action. I guess I'm the kind of person who doesn't appreciate the sunshine until it's gone.

"I've added a new component to your therapy," Dr. Deb says to me one afternoon toward the end of February. I knew this day was coming, when we'd run out of therapy games to play and the real talking would have to begin, and I've dreaded it.

"What is it?" I ask her cautiously.

"Why don't we go take a look? Grab your jacket."

I have several jackets that I pile on top of one another. I use my socks for mittens, even though my dad bought me a pair of gloves—I can never seem to find them. He also sent me a faux fur–lined hat with earflaps that I wear whenever I'm outdoors. In Dr. Deb's office I pile on my ragtag winter gear and follow her outside. It's bitterly cold, but by the time we've crossed the lawn, I'm starting to warm up. And truthfully, I'd rather be outside in the frozen tundra than inside the mind factory with the cinder-block walls and wheezing heater. I follow Dr. Deb past the school building and down the hill, heading toward the maintenance shed, though I'm not sure why. I notice a guy on the lawn, shoveling dirt, then stop because I recognize him—it's A.J.

"What's he doing here?"

"We're introducing a new therapy at Sunny Meadows," Dr. Deb says, "and we've chosen two residents to be part of our pilot program. We're calling it 'garden therapy.'"

I glance over at A.J. and realize she means the two of us. *Oh no.* I can be cooperative up to a point, but not this. Not him.

"I don't know anything about gardening," I say. It's the truth. My grandmother once had a garden, but I was little then. I can't remember the first thing to do.

Dr. Deb doesn't answer me but continues on with her spiel. "By agreeing to participate in our pilot program with A.J., you'll have to forgo one of your therapy sessions per week and two of your group activities."

In any other circumstance I'd be jumping for joy. But not in this case. "I can't even keep a houseplant alive," I say, but I don't think she's listening.

"Your rehabilitative team has agreed to reward you with a special privilege for your participation."

"What privilege is that?" I ask. I've gotten so used to living without privileges, I doubt they'll be able to sway me.

Dr. Deb pulls something out of her pocket. My MP3 player. I almost don't recognize it, it's been so long. But more than my music, that player represents the real me. The person I know and understand.

"Of course, you can't listen to it at school or in therapy," she says, "but any other time . . ."

I glance over at A.J., who can't hear us but is watching nonetheless. He sees the prize in Dr. Deb's hand. He knows

I'm being bribed. Maybe he's been bribed as well. I don't see how he'd agree to it otherwise.

If I say no to this therapy, my efforts will count for nothing. My team will know I'm still the old Taylor—defiant and stubborn. And my release date—if it even exists—will be pushed back further.

But if I agree to it, then they can't help but document it as progress. I'm cooperating and participating, as long as I can get along with A.J.

"Okay," I say at last.

"Great," Dr. Deb says. "A safety will be making rounds to check up on you two. For now, good luck."

She turns to go.

"Wait, where are you going?" With her around, at least I know things won't get too personal. Part of therapy is the therapist, right?

"Oh, that's the best part of this program," Dr. Deb says with a smile. "It's resident-led."

She walks away, and I know that this has all been one big setup. That must be what rehabilitative teams do—get together and think of the worst possible situations they can and then make it part of your "program."

I turn back to A.J., who's resumed digging, and see that he's scraping up the top layer of brown sod, in foot-long strips, and depositing it nearby.

"What are you doing?" I ask, because I have no idea where to begin.

"Making rows for the beds," he says without looking over.

Maybe I should be doing the same thing. I don't need to ask him where the shovels are. I planted enough trees over winter break to know my way around the maintenance shed. I walk in there and grab myself a shovel. Under normal circumstances, they probably wouldn't let us around this kind of equipment, but the Chain Gang was going in and out of the shed all the time and no one got decapitated, so I guess in that way we earned their trust. Maybe that's part of why they chose us for this pilot program. Not that I believe that's what this is. Not at all.

I take the socks off my hands, find a spot far away from A.J., and start digging up the grass. A few minutes later, he's standing over me. I'd forgotten how tall he is. Maybe he's grown since the last time I saw him.

"You're too far away," he says.

"Does it really matter?" I say in a huff.

He walks back to the shed, picks up the entire length of hose, throws it over one shoulder, then comes back to me, unraveling it along the way. The hose stops about ten feet away from where I stand.

"Going to be pretty hard to water."

I drop my shovel and stalk over to the pieces of sod, mad

that he's right about this, too. I pick up the clumps of grass one by one and drop them back into place as he stands by, watching me with an amused expression, which only irritates me more.

"Why don't you just tell me where you want the rows?" I say. "Since *you* have to be the one in charge."

He raises his eyebrows at this. "Is that right?"

"That's been my experience."

He crosses his arms. "Maybe," he says slowly, "if you'd told me what you were planning to do *before* you did it, I could have saved you a lot of trouble."

I respond bitterly, because I know we're no longer talking about the garden, but about what happened between us. "I guess I forgot how *helpful* and *considerate* you are."

He shakes his head and walks over to where his shovel lies on the ground, plucks it up, and heads for the shed. He comes out a minute later empty-handed and wraps up the hose.

"Don't forget to put your tools away when you leave," he says as he passes by. I glare at his back as he walks up the hill. He's probably on his way to get me kicked out of the program. Tattle on me again. Or maybe he'll quit and they'll find someone else to take his place, which would be super. Anyone else I could fake being nice to.

But not him.

CHAPTER 16

A.J.'s out there again the next garden day. I should have known it wouldn't be that easy to get rid of him. I find my shovel where I left it in the shed and resume work on the row I began the last time, which is as far away as I can possibly get from him and still be within the hose's reach.

"I thought you quit," I say in place of hello.

"Sorry to disappoint you."

Disappointed indeed, especially when I see that he's finished up two rows to my one. I take off one of my jackets and set to digging, but it's hard work. And these sod patches are heavy.

"Why don't you take a break?" he says to me. "I'll finish this one for you."

"I got it," I say, even though my hands are starting to blister. I don't need his help.

"You don't have to be so damn stubborn."

I glare up at him. "You don't have to be so damn bossy."

"Are we ever going to get past this?"

"Get past what?"

"You being mad at me."

"Who says I'm mad? To be mad, I'd have to care. And I don't."

He shakes his head and walks away. Just when I think he might be leaving again, he turns and laps the beds, coming to a stop in the same exact place in front of me.

"All right," he says. "Let's just get it out now. Whatever you have to say to me, do it and let's be done."

I throw down my shovel and plant my hands on my hips. It's been a long time coming. "Did you know the whole time you were going to rat me out?"

His bravado falters a little.

"No."

"When was it, then?"

He rakes one hand through his hair, his nervous twitch. "That day on the lawn when you fainted and I carried you up to the infirmary. You were so helpless and weak. I mean, you couldn't even *breathe*, Taylor."

He carried me? I never knew that. I just assumed a safety had taken me. I never knew my episode had affected him at all. Even so, he didn't have to do what he did.

"And then I saw your father with you and I started thinking." He rubs his forehead, leaving a dirt smudge on his sweaty skin. "You have someone who really cares about you and wants you to get better. I should have never given you that key. But by then it was too late." He lifts his eyes to meet mine. "You tell me. In the basement, when you said you'd stay until December. Did you mean it?"

I swallow hard. There's no sense in lying. "No."

He nods his head. "Yeah, that's what I thought."

We stand there a moment longer, staring at each other in silence. Then he picks up his shovel and goes back to digging. I do the same, squeezing the handle with all my anger and frustration, but worse than that is the guilt. The pain in my hands feels good, like a punishment I deserve. I don't quit until I've got three rows completed. They're not nearly as straight or as tidy as his, but neither am I.

When I finally lay down my shovel, the throbbing in my hands is so bad its creeping up my arms. He grabs both my hands and turns them over. My palms and fingers are red, and some of the blisters have already grown white, puffy heads.

"Stubborn," he says, and drops my hands, then picks up my shovel to put it away for me. I walk up the hill without him. At the top I look back to see our six unmatched rows. His are straight and even. Mine look like the claw mark of a wild animal.

"How's garden therapy going?" Dr. Deb asks me the following week, our first session since the garden began.

"Great," I say with a happy, happy chirp to my voice.

"How are you and A.J. getting along?"

"Super-duper."

"That's wonderful. In a few weeks, I'll be asking you both to fill out evaluations, so that we can go over them in your respective team meetings."

I stop and replay her words in my head. "Are you saying A.J. is part of my team?"

She smiles. "Consider it more like a peer review."

That means A.J. can say whatever he wants about me—it doesn't even have to be true—and my rehabilitative team will have to consider it. That's *so* not fair.

"Have you been practicing your breathing?" she asks. She glances at my fist, which is knuckling my chest—I do it without thinking. I shove my hands in my pockets so they won't betray me.

"Every night," I tell her, but really it's been so long that I've forgotten the words.

"Good, then I think we're ready to talk about what happens when you can't breathe."

"What do you mean?"

"Your father described them as your episodes."

The feeling is what she wants to know about. I glance at the walls that confine us; the heat keeps coming on and making it stuffy and difficult to breathe. I wish we could go outside for a minute. Just to get some fresh air.

"Can we do this outside?" I ask her.

"Therapy?"

"I mean, I guess it doesn't matter."

"No, I think that's an excellent idea. Let's do it."

We bundle up and head outdoors. At the crest of the hill I look down and see A.J. in the garden, using a wheelbarrow and pitchfork to make piles of something.

"What's he doing down there?" I say suspiciously.

"You don't know?"

"No, I just thought he was going to wait for me. You know, everything together, right?"

Dr. Deb raises one eyebrow, and I glance back at the garden. He better not be trying to fix my rows. I spot a picnic bench off to the side, far enough away that he can't hear us, but close enough that I can keep an eye on him. "Why don't we go sit over there?" I say to Dr. Deb.

"Sounds good to me."

We settle down at the bench. A.J. glances our way, and I nod to let him know I'm watching.

"We were discussing your episodes," Dr. Deb says. "How long have you been having them?"

"A while," I say as if it's no big deal.

"Do you remember when they first began?"

"No," I say, which is a lie. I remember exactly when they began, the night the police found me alone in my mom's car and then took her away. It's the feeling of the policeman's arms, confining me, holding me back, only it has somehow morphed over the years, so that it's no longer just on the outside, but on the inside, too. Just thinking about it makes me feel shaky and weak.

"Can you describe it for me?" she says.

"Describe what?"

"How it feels."

The feeling will go away eventually. I'll outgrow it, like an allergy. I don't want to explain it. Talking about it only makes it worse.

"I'd rather not," I say.

"If you try, then maybe I can help you understand it. We can figure this out together."

I have to let her think she's helping. Otherwise, she won't feel as though she's done her job. One thing I've learned about Dr. Deb—she's no quitter.

"I'm only explaining it once," I say.

She nods. "Okay."

"It starts here." I point to my chest. "It gets really tight, like a fist crushing me, then it feels like hands around my throat. Sometimes I get nauseous, too, and these weird hot flashes, dizzy spells. My heart beats so fast and it's hard to . . . catch my breath."

I stop talking, because I feel tremors of the feeling starting up. I rub my chest, and she waits for me to continue. When I don't, she only nods. "It sounds to me like what you're describing is what's known as a panic attack."

Panic attack. I've heard that name before, but somehow it never applied to me. Still, that describes it precisely. Panic. Attack.

"Isn't there some pill I can take for it?" If there were, I would take it. Then we could skip therapy altogether.

"There are medications that can be prescribed for anxiety, but they don't always target the problem as specifically as we'd like. The interesting thing about panic attacks is that they're brought on by an initial fear or trigger, which intensifies during the attack, forming a positive feedback loop."

"A what?"

"A positive feedback loop is where A produces more of B, which in turn produces more of A. In other words, a kind of downward spiral."

"But what causes it?" I ask her.

"You do. Your phobias. Your fears."

I'm the one causing it? I mean, I know it comes from inside me, but I thought it was some sort of chemical imbalance, like depression or ADHD. It's not like I'm imagining it . . . am I?

"Are you telling me it's all in my head?"

"Yes, but that's not to say it's not very real. Panic attacks are some of the most intensely frightening, upsetting, and uncomfortable experiences of a person's life. Many people who've had them describe it as feeling like they're going crazy or leaving their body. Have you ever felt that way?"

"No," I say, a lie. Why can't I just be honest with her? Maybe because it means admitting something I'm not ready for. That I might be the kind of crazy that can't be fixed.

Dr. Deb sits back. I avoid her eyes and stare at A.J. instead. I wish I were over there instead of here. Anything would be better than this right now.

"Why don't you tell me about the first time you had a panic attack?" Dr. Deb says.

"I told you, I can't remember."

"Try, Taylor."

"You're not listening to me."

"I *am* listening to you. I'm listening to everything you say as well as everything you *don't* say."

I look up at her. A helpless feeling washes over me.

"How old were you?"

"Nine."

"Where were you?"

"In front of a bar."

"What were you doing there?"

"I was watching my mom get arrested." I feel the cop's arms wrap around me, squeezing me while I screamed at them to let her go, to let me go with her. I really was splitting in two. Because they were taking my mother away from me.

The feeling starts up like I'm nine years old all over again. Dr. Deb tells me to breathe, but I can't because the policeman is squeezing me so tight and my mother, when she looks at me, I see the fear in her eyes and it only makes me more afraid. They're taking her away, and I might never see her again. And it's all my fault, because I told on her. *I told.*

I stand and circle a small patch of lawn like a wounded bird, round and round without stopping, until I'm so dizzy I think I might fall over. I kneel on the ground and watch my shallow breath cloud in the air above me.

"Deep breath in," Dr. Deb says. I take a deep breath and hold it. "Now exhale slowly, counting as you do. I am powerful. I am strong. I am in control."

I count backwards in my head—*ten, nine, eight* . . . I tell myself this feeling will pass . . . *three, two, one.* I take another deep breath, and this one breaks through and rushes into my chest, expanding it, loosening it up. I breathe in, exhale out, and count. I say the words in my head. After a few more cycles, the feeling passes.

"Practice your breathing every night," she says.

"I do," I say irritably.

She looks at me doggedly. "Then practice it twice."

I sit up in the grass, ready to go.

"Are we done here?"

"Not yet," she says. "Your team met yesterday. We'd like to offer you the opportunity to be a peer mentor to a new resident."

"Me?" I ask, and point at myself dumbly. First the garden and now this. They keep adding things to the list.

"We think it'll be a good exercise for you. If you do a good job, you'll be that much closer to accomplishing your rehabilitative goals."

Rehabilitative goals . . . the carrot they dangle in front of my nose to keep me doing the things I don't want to do.

"What if I don't want to?" I ask her.

"You can always say no," she says without finishing. She doesn't need to. If my team says to do it, I do it. Otherwise, I can sit in here and rot.

"Fine," I say. "I'll do it."

I am strong. I am powerful. I am in control.

Yeah, right.

CHAPTER 17

I leave our therapy session and promptly forget about the peer mentorship thing, that is, until that weekend in the dorms when I hear the screaming.

In the hallway I catch sight of a new girl, who can only be my new mentee, since Dr. Deb said she'd be arriving this weekend and staying on the second floor. Her hair's been dyed pink, but her brown roots are showing. She's skinny—all knees and elbows—and looks like a giraffe as she jumps awkwardly, screaming at Rhonda to "Give it back!" Rhonda holds what I can only guess is her cell phone above their heads and it's ringing, which seems to be driving the girl absolutely insane.

"No cell phones," Rhonda says sternly, and I know she has no intention of giving it back.

"This is worse than a dictatorship!" the girl shouts. "You people are all commie bastards." She whirls around and stomps down the hall, then attempts to slam her door shut, but it's impossible because the doors are all hinged with air locks. Rhonda is one step behind her, opening the door wide and reminding her that "Privacy is a privilege."

"Suck my dick!" the girl shouts loud enough for everyone on the floor to hear. I watch Rhonda's profile to see if she'll react, but she decides to let this one go. By this time, the other girls have scattered to their own rooms like roaches in the light. On the second floor, they avoid trouble at all costs.

I need Margo. She would know how to handle this girl. But Margo's not here, and I have to figure this one out on my own.

This isn't the ideal time to meet her, but if I wait for the perfect moment, it might never come. I'm supposed to introduce myself. That's the first step. The sooner I get this mentorship started, the sooner I reach my "rehabilitative goals."

I give her a few minutes to cool off and then head to her room. I step loudly so she knows I'm coming and stop in her doorway. I don't know where she comes from or what she's been through, but I can probably guess at how she's feeling right now—trapped, alone, frustrated, scared.

"What do you want?" she asks with a sour glare, but I see the fear beneath it.

"My name's Taylor," I say. "I'm your . . ." I clear my throat. It sounds so stupid out loud. "Peer mentor."

Her upper lip curls in disgust. "Really?" she asks, testing me to see if I'll back down. If I'm going to be her mentor, I need her to like me. Or at least, not hate me.

"Yeah," I say. "Really."

Her eyes narrow to slits. "Then do us both a favor and *fuck off.*"

"Maybe we could—"

"I said FUCK OFF!"

On my way back to my room, I realize my team has given me a nearly impossible task, much like garden therapy. But I'm not going to give them a reason to keep me here. This new girl is going to get some mentoring, whether she wants it or not.

The next day in the pen I'm sitting in my usual corner with my chemistry textbook, trying to balance some chemical equations while Charlotte colors blissfully at my side, when I see the new girl again. McKenzie is her name, and she's the new buzz among residents. Today, like yesterday, she's screaming at the safety. *"Give them back!"* she screeches, along with more colorful four-letter words. This time, it's her cigarettes. Even without Victor, the Sunny Meadows black market thrives.

I know what's going to happen next. McKenzie is going to do something stupid and get herself thrown into a time-out room, which is only going to make her feel more angry and alone. I *am* her peer mentor, so I get up and pull an A.J., stepping right between her and the safety. The safety takes a step back, which is monumental in itself. And I've startled McKenzie long enough to interrupt her steady stream of profanities.

"Hey, new girl," I say to her. Her eyes focus on mine, and I see an unbridled anger in them that is so familiar. "Why don't you try being a little less obvious next time? There are a lot of other places you can smoke your cigarettes." I jerk my thumb to the safety at my back. "And screaming doesn't have any effect on these guys. They're not even human. They're robot clones sent here to terrorize us and make our lives a living hell. So save your screaming for therapy, because that's when you're really going to need it."

She lowers her arms, and instead of glaring at the safety, she glares at me. "I told you to fuck off," she says, and storms off toward the door. Another safety blocks her exit, and she actually kicks the guy in the shin. I've got to give her points for that. Of course they immediately take hold of her and drag her kicking and screaming out of the pen, no doubt on her way to a little R & R on the first floor.

Some people just have to learn the hard way.

I walk back over to Charlotte, thinking that at least I tried to keep her out of trouble. "McKenzie needs a coloring book," Charlotte says with a happy little smile on her face.

"That girl needs two."

But Charlotte's observation gives me an idea, so that

afternoon before I head down to the garden, I pick up my newest coloring book, one that Dr. Deb ordered for me online. It's superheroes—all female. I haven't even gotten the chance to color one myself, but I do now. The very first page is Wonder Woman, who was always my favorite as a kid, because even though she's not Indian, her hair is black like mine and she can talk to animals and she's got that sweet golden tiara that doubles as a razor-sharp boomerang, which is the best use of a tiara, ever. I color that page, and on the bottom I write her a dedication. *To: McKenzie, From: Taylor.*

I leave it on her bed with my pack of crayons, thinking I'll have to borrow some from Charlotte or get another pack of my own. Then I head for the garden. It's my first time down since I saw A.J. messing around in there without me. I inspect his piles, which look to be a mixture of grass clippings, wood chips, and food scraps. There's an oily banana skin in one, and I remember when I was a little girl at my grandmother's house, putting my banana peels in a glass jar that she said was for compost.

"Don't look too long," he says, surprising me. I glance at him with annoyance and then back at his piles, where I recognize bits of eggshell and used coffee filters.

"Are you sure all that stuff's supposed to be in there?"

"Darlin'," he says with a syrupy drawl, "this *ain't* my first rodeo."

I roll my eyes. He never misses an opportunity to remind me how *knowledgeable* and *experienced* he is.

"If we let it sit long enough, it'll be good for planting," he says. "Better than the dirt we have here."

"What's wrong with this dirt?"

He reaches into one of the beds and pulls out a fistful of red clay. "Not enough drainage or nutrients."

"Where'd you get all this stuff?"

"Scraps from the kitchen. Clippings from maintenance. Wood from a ground-up tree stump."

I eye the piles again. He sure is resourceful.

"We can share it," he says.

"No, that's all right. I'll make my own."

He snorts and shakes his head. "Of course you will. So, I guess this is going to be your side then." He motions to my three bedraggled rows with an air of superiority. But at least they're mine, carved out of the earth by my own blistered hands.

"Yeah, this is my side."

"Tell me, when's the last time you put in a garden?"

"I'll figure it out. I mean, how hard can it be?"

He gives me a sideways glance.

"Well, you've got your rows and I've got mine," I say. "Why don't we just see whose garden grows better?"

"Fine, but you're at a disadvantage."

"Oh, really?" He thinks I can't do it without him. "You willing to bet on that?"

He scratches his chin. "That depends. What're the stakes?"

I think of the evaluations we'll have to fill out in a few weeks. I need A.J. to give Dr. Deb a glowing report. And I'm more likely to beat him in a bet than convince him on my own that I deserve it.

"If I win," I say, "you have to tell Dr. Deb that I'm the most well-adjusted, friendly, and cooperative person you've ever worked with. You tell her that garden therapy is a huge success, largely thanks to me."

He raises his eyebrows. "That's a pretty tall order. And if I win?"

"Then I'll do the same."

He scratches his chin, seeming to consider it. "Well, the thing is, I'm going to be in here until I'm eighteen, no matter what you tell Dr. Deb."

"Then what do you want?"

"How about we try being friends?"

"I'm not that good of an actress," I say, then see from the wounded look in his eyes I've gone too far. I feel bad, but I don't apologize. You can't force someone to be your friend.

He shakes his head and points at the dorms. "You know, a few minutes ago I was up there looking down here at you, thinking back to when I *thought* I liked you. But now, I can't seem to remember why."

I stare at the ground so that I don't have to look at him. He walks away, and I pick up my hoe and hack up the dirt. My blisters still haven't healed all the way, but I attack the ground with everything I have. With A.J., there's no way to win.

I spend my next few therapy sessions practicing the breathing with Dr. Deb. I don't understand why she's so focused on this exercise, but at least I don't have to talk. She makes me say the mantra aloud, too. Not just a whisper, but *loud and clear.*

"I am powerful," I practically shout at her. "I am strong. I am in control."

It's pretty ridiculous.

On garden days I collect scraps for my compost. A.J. and I have split up the week to make it fair. He collects from the kitchen on Monday through Wednesday and I collect Thursday through Saturday. Sundays we divide it between us. I've also started raking up oak leaves to add to the mix. We're both so busy that we hardly talk or look at each other, and it suits me just fine. After a week of tilling up my rows with a rake and a hoe, I'm ready to plant my first seeds. So, at my next therapy session, I tell Dr. Deb.

"You're ready to plant already?" she asks me. "It's not even March yet."

"Spring is right around the corner." The sooner I've got a garden, the sooner we can call garden therapy a success.

She tilts her head. "What does A.J. say about it?"

Who cares what A.J. says?

"He's behind me all the way."

"Well, I'll see what I can get from the nursery in town."

A couple of days later she gives me the packets of seeds, and I take them down to the garden straightaway. A.J.'s there already, using a pitchfork to turn over his compost. He's also got a short plastic barrel, filled with what, I have no idea.

"What's in there?" I ask.

"Take a look," he says, and lifts the lid off the container. He reaches in, pushing aside food scraps and black muck, digging deep. He pulls out his filthy arm and opens his fist to show me a handful of wriggling red worms.

"Oh, gross," I say, and back up quick.

"These beauties are going to turn my soil into black gold."

"I thought black gold was oil."

"Well, you know. What's that you got there?"

I open my paper bag to show him my packs of seeds—carrots, tomatoes, peas, and cucumbers.

"Little early to be planting. I'd wait till after the freeze if I were you."

"There's no harm in trying," I say, because I'm tired of him telling me what to do.

I use a stick to make little pits for the seeds, then drop a couple in and cover them back up. While I do it, I hear my grandmother's voice in my head.

Now tuck them in, Taylor, and tell them good night.

After I've planted all three rows and made little wooden labels for them, I stand back and survey my work. A.J. glances over. "You going to water them in or wait for the rain?"

I never thought about that, and I don't know how much or how often to water them.

"Wait for the rain," I say.

He nods. "Good idea."

I don't know if I've given him the right answer, but he seems to trust me enough to decide for myself.

I glance up to see him smiling at me. Without thinking, I smile back.

I'm in independent study the next day when a safety brings McKenzie in, somewhat forcefully. She must have gotten kicked out of her therapy elective, since everyone in here seems to be a therapy dropout.

She plops down in the chair across from mine. I glance up to find her staring at me.

"What is it?" I ask her. I'm exhausted. There aren't enough hours in the day for all this schoolwork, much less McKenzie's drama. Besides, my words of wisdom in the pen don't seem to have done her any good.

"I hear you're the girl who tried to escape."

"Yeah," I say without enthusiasm. I'll live on in infamy in the halls of Sunny Meadows as the girl who tried to run away, got caught, lost her mind, and lived to tell the tale.

Her eyes light up. "I heard your boyfriend made you the key to one of the shop cars."

Why do people insist on linking the two of us together? Still?

"He's not my boyfriend."

She leans forward and lowers her voice. "Does he still make keys?"

"I don't know. It's not something we talk about."

"Maybe I should ask him."

I shrug as if I don't care. If she's anything like me, trying to talk her out of it will only make her go harder. But there is something that might make her pause.

"I guess you never heard the second part of the story."

"What's that?"

"He's also the one who ratted me out."

"Burn," she says, and sits back, considering it for a moment.

Then she gets up and pokes around the room, looking over the other kids' shoulders and being a general nuisance until Ms. Sylvia tells her to go sit back down.

"Anyway, here," she says, and tosses me a folded-up piece of paper. I open it up and see that she's been coloring from my book. This one is Poison Ivy with flames for hair. McKenzie's also drawn in her own weaponry, a green mace-looking thing with rainbow-hued lasers coming out on all sides.

And at the bottom she's written, *To: Taylor, From: McKenzie.*

"They have art therapy, you know."

She shrugs. "I'm still exploring other options."

I bet she is. "Let me know how that works out. After all, I am your peer mentor."

"Yeah. Maybe I will."

After school that day I go down to the garden. Halfway down the hill I notice A.J. planted like a scarecrow in the middle of the rows, watching my descent. As I get closer, I see that he's an angry scarecrow with a face that would scare even the butterflies away. He doesn't wait for me to ask him what's wrong.

"Why'd you tell McKenzie about the key?" he says.

"I didn't know it was a secret."

He shakes his head. "I don't make keys anymore. I learned my lesson with you. As if the time I spent on the first floor wasn't enough."

"They put you in a time-out?" That doesn't seem fair. It's not like *he* tried to escape.

"Of course they did. You didn't think they'd let me get away with it, did you?"

I take a step back, because there is real anger behind his words. I watch him walk away, heading for the shed. I never wished for him to be punished like that. I feel pretty rotten about it—the whole thing. When he comes back out, I try again.

"Listen, A.J., for what it's worth, I told McKenzie it was a bad idea. But with her, it's like talking to a wall. She's going to do what she's going to do."

He chuckles without any humor and says, "They found you a good one. She sounds just like you."

"I'm not . . ." I trail off, because I can't find the words to finish.

He gestures at the space between us. "You know, I just wish . . ." He shakes his head and won't look at me. "I wish it didn't have to be so damn hard."

He walks away before I can say anything else. I watch him climb the hill. He doesn't look back.

CHAPTER 18

It rains for the next few days. The drip, Tabitha calls it, when it rains all day long, just enough to keep you inside. It's good for my seeds, at least. Maybe on the other side of this rain, there will be a rainbow and the promise of some new shoots in the garden.

I walk into Dr. Deb's office that week, and she throws me yet another curveball.

"I'd like your permission to have your father join us today."

I glance around her office, wondering where he could be hiding. "Um, okay."

She punches her computer keyboard, then angles the monitor so that we both can see it. "Welcome, Mr. Truwell."

I'm face-to-face with my dad. I try my best to smile. To my surprise, he smiles back.

"Hi, Taylor," he says.

"Hi, Dad."

"You look well."

I nod my head. "I feel . . . well."

"Dr. Deb sent me pictures of the garden you and A.J. have been working on. It looks promising. How is that going?"

I think back to my most recent encounter with A.J. That part of it, not so good, but the rest, not too bad.

"I planted my first seeds."

"Already?" he asks. "It's still cold up there, isn't it?"

"It's getting warmer. And look, it's raining today. So maybe they'll sprout soon."

"That's wonderful," he says. "Your grandmother would be proud."

I stop and feel the weight of his words. I haven't done anything to make my grandmother proud in a long time.

"How's school going?" he asks.

At last, a subject I don't have to fake. "I'm making up the work I missed. And I built a bookshelf for one of my teachers. He's got this awesome collection of biographies. He lent me one about Chief Osceola. It's pretty good, actually."

My dad smiles. "This is good, Taylor. I'm pleased to see you're really trying."

I nod, but for some reason his praise makes me uncomfortable instead of proud.

He asks me a few more questions about school, and our conversation ends pleasantly enough. I realize as I'm walking out of Dr. Deb's office that the real me could never have done that—talk to my dad without arguing—but the fake me could. How sad is that?

When the rain stops, I go back to the garden to find my first new shoots poking through the ground. I'm so excited I want to jump up and shout it out loud, but instead I go around and collect stones, then pile them up at the head of one row as a dedication to my grandmother.

I spend that day turning my compost with a pitchfork. In the middle of the heap, the compost is steamy and warm, and I remember A.J.'s words, *Got to let it cook.* Below that, I'm amazed to find that it's turned to rich black compost. I check on his worm bin and feed them some scraps from the kitchen. As I'm replacing the lid, a black racer slithers by. I recall my grandmother's story of Rabbit, who outwitted Snake by challenging him to prove his length by tying himself in a knot. When Snake did, Rabbit ran away.

It's been happening a lot lately. Stories and songs I thought were lost forever keep popping back into my mind. Maybe they needed the right setting to come back to me. Maybe they've been there all along.

That night there's a frost warning on TV, and I worry about my baby plants. After school the next day I rush down to the garden to check on them and see, to my surprise, that someone has covered my rows with burlap sacks.

A.J.

I uncover the rows and see the shoots still green and standing. They've weathered the cold, because of his care and attention. Looking down at the new seedlings, I start to feel really bad about the way I've treated him. I don't want to fight with him anymore.

"Thanks for doing that," I tell him, folding the sacks and putting them back in the shed.

"I wanted to give you—I mean, the plants—a fighting chance."

"Well . . . I appreciate it."

He nods and stares at me a moment longer. I suddenly miss our friendship. And how we could tell each other anything. But too much has happened between us.

Even if I knew the words to fix it, I don't know how to say them.

That week in therapy Dr. Deb begins our session by telling me we're going to focus on my anxiety issues.

"What anxiety issues?"

She doesn't answer but instead hands me a legal pad and pen. "I'd like you to list your fears on this piece of paper."

"I don't have any," I say, and try to give it back. She holds up her hand to stop me.

"Maybe you're afraid to list them," she says. "That's Fear number one."

"That's ridiculous," I say. Is Dr. Deb calling me a chicken? She motions to the pad in front of me. "Fine." I grip the pen tighter. "I'll do it."

I put the pen to the paper and stare at the page until the lines blur. Finally I begin writing, listing every fear I can think of—flying, falling, dying, drowning, along with some I've picked up from Charlotte, such as dropping a toothbrush on the bathroom floor, and one of McKenzie's—flying monkeys.

When I'm finished, I hand it back to Dr. Deb.

"Well, Taylor," she says with a wry smile. "I think you've listed every fear on here except your own."

The real me can't help but scowl at her.

"I'm giving you until our next session to come up with *your* list," she says. "After all, you want to be rehabilitated, don't you?"

I glare at her without answering, but she only smiles.

After my session I carry the legal pad wherever I go. I want to just do it and get it over with, but every time I try to write something down, I can't. My fears are sleeping vipers. If I wake them, they might attack, and then I'll be worse off than before.

I'm down in the garden the next day with my baby shoots, which are sadly turning yellow with brown, crumbly tips—I think the cold may have affected them in spite of A.J.'s blankets. I heard somewhere that talking to plants helps them grow, so instead of working on Dr. Deb's assignment, I sit down in the middle of a row and sing one of my grandmother's songs, a chant that her mother taught her—a prayer of safety for when the men left the village to go hunting. That song reminds me of another and another. I've forgotten some of the words, but the melodies are there, in my bones. The singing warms my chest and helps me breathe, and the more I do it, the clearer her voice becomes in my mind—deep like a river, rich like soil, soulful and real. It's as if she's sitting there beside me.

I stop when I see A.J. approaching.

"Hey," he calls to me.

"Hey, yourself."

He goes about his business of spreading compost over his rows and I watch him, pen in hand, blank page in front of me.

"What are you working on?" he asks.

"Oh, nothing. Just some assignment."

"For school?"

"No. Therapy."

"Ah," he says, and drops it. There's a kind of unwritten rule at Sunny Meadows that you don't discuss therapy. It's the one thing that doesn't get talked about. I think about something A.J. said to me in the beginning, how he'd be the same person out there as he is in here. A.J. believes in therapy and in being rehabilitated. But maybe he has to, because he's been here for so long.

"Is therapy ever . . . hard for you?" I ask him.

He sets down his shovel and looks over at me. "Nearly every time."

"Do you think it's worth it?" He looks uncertain. I try again. "I mean, do you think you're getting better?"

"I hope so."

I believe him. That he wants to be better. But do *I*? I glance down at the paper. What is stopping me? It's not A.J. or my father or Dr. Deb. I can't even blame my mother for this one. It's me. I am the only one keeping me from getting better.

I begin to write, a small trickle at first, then a wide, gushing stream. There's so many I have to turn the page over and write on the back. It's overwhelming, how many fears I have.

A drip on the page smears the ink, and I realize I'm crying.

"Here." I glance up to see A.J. offering me one of his sweat rags. "It's clean. Mostly."

I wipe my eyes with it and catch a whiff of his scent. It reminds me of his hugs—so warm and comforting. I could use one of those hugs right now, but I've been such a bitch to him, over and over.

"Thanks," I say, and hand it back to him.

"Keep it. I've got more."

Later that night in my dorm room, I sleep with his rag pressed against my pillow. His pine-needle scent reminds me of home.

That week I come down with a cold that keeps me in my dorm room for the next few days. This means I don't have to go to school or therapy or the garden, where I know my plants have shriveled up and died. I don't have to face Dr. Deb or A.J. or my own mounting flaws. The fear list sits on my desk, taunting me. I've already mentally added another one.

Fear Number 37: Showing this list to someone else.

The advantage to being dorm-bound is that I've had a lot of time for schoolwork, and I've been able to hang out more with McKenzie. We're in the common area going over her geometry homework when the phone rings, surprising both of us. For a second we just stare at each other, not knowing what to do.

"I better answer it," she says. I watch her puzzled expression as she picks up the phone, then says to me, "It's for you. Some girl named Margo?"

Margo. After all this time she hasn't forgotten about me. Will she be mad at me for not calling?

"Margo?" I say into the telephone.

"Taylor, oh my God. Why haven't you called me?"

"I don't know. I guess I've just been . . . busy."

And I have been busy, but the real reason is that I was afraid she might not want to talk to me. She's on the outside now, living life, while I'm still in here.

"That hurts my feelings, T," she says. "I should be your first priority."

I smile. I can almost see her pouting in front of me right now.

"How are you, Margo? Where—are you?"

"I'm fairly fabulous. I'm living with my aunt in Manhattan. I can stand in the middle of my bedroom and touch the opposite walls. My wardrobe has been utterly decimated, but that's not even the worst of it."

"What's wrong?" What could possibly be worse for Margo than having to downsize her wardrobe?

She sighs dramatically. "I had to dye my hair brown."

I smile at that. "But Margo, you're a natural blonde."

"I know, I know, but I got this part in a play. I'm supposed to be the smart, bookish type, and apparently, blondes can't read."

"Wow, Margo, that's awesome. You're really doing it."

"Yes, I am. But I miss you. And Victor."

"How *is* Victor?"

"He's fabulous. He's coming to visit me this summer, and

I can hardly wait. It's strange, all the new people I meet . . . it's like they don't really *know* me. I never thought I'd say this, but sometimes, I even miss the Latina Queens."

I laugh at that. "You must be feeling pretty sentimental."

"I guess I am." She giggles, and it's like wind chimes in the breeze. Hearing her voice on the phone, I realize just how much I've missed her. I should have called her a long time ago.

"But tell me about you, T. How are you doing?"

"Much better. I had a rough couple of months."

"A.J. told me about it."

A.J.? I didn't know they talked. But she did give him that note to give to me, with her numbers on it.

"Do you guys talk . . . a lot?"

"Enough. We have something in common now."

"What's that?"

"You, silly."

"Oh. Right." I don't know to feel about it.

"He's so different than I thought, T. And when he talks about you . . . he really cares."

I suddenly feel like I'm on the outside. What exactly do they talk about? It seems like any story he'd tell about me would be a bad one.

"So what else is new in Sunny Meadows?" she asks. "How are the Latina Queens?"

I tell her about how they're not a gang anymore, how

Brandi and I made up, sort of. How Charlotte and I have become friends.

"And get this, they made me a peer mentor."

"Really?"

"Yeah. Her name is McKenzie." I glance over at her; she's sticking her tongue out at me. "We're a lot alike."

I ask Margo what's going on in her life, and she tells me about her play director, who's an insane egomaniac, and the stage manager, who throws tantrums whenever Margo doesn't put something back exactly where she found it. And her costar, who's a worse kleptomaniac than she is. "He's a *guy*, Taylor, and he's stealing my makeup. I swear I'm on my fifth tube of mascara. I think I'm going to have to sabotage him with Krazy Glue. Then at least I'll have proof of it."

She gets me laughing like I haven't in a while. Our conversation isn't nearly long enough, but I have to let her go because there are other girls waiting for their turn with the phone.

"Listen, T," she says as we're saying our good-byes. "I know you and A.J. still have some things to work out. But maybe you guys could give it another chance."

"Maybe," I say with uncertainty.

I tell her good-bye, and as I'm hanging up the phone I remember something my grandmother once told me, how we express our love by actions, not words. With A.J. words fail me, but maybe with actions, I can make things right between us.

CHAPTER 19

The weekend passes, and when Monday comes, I can't milk my cold anymore. I'm back in school, which means back in therapy and back in the garden. It's the middle of March now, and the new leaves are beginning to unfurl themselves like the ribbons of pretty packages. Something else is happening too. When I smile at people, I can no longer tell if it's the real me or the fake me. It's like my two personalities are somehow fusing into one. And in class, when I'm answering questions, it doesn't feel like I'm faking it anymore. It's just . . . me.

"Better watch yourself, Taylor," Brandi says to me in the hall that day. "People are going to think you like it in here."

"Hardly." School is decent and dorm living is getting better, but if there's one thing I'll never get used to, it's the part where you have to spill your guts.

In therapy that afternoon I have the fear list in my pocket, but I'm afraid to show it to Dr. Deb—Fear Number 37.

"It's been a while since I last saw you," she says.

"Yeah, I was, um, sick." I cough a little into my hand.

232 | COUNTING BACKWARDS

"I'm glad to see that you're feeling better. Do you have the list?"

I dig it out of my pocket and hand it over. Dr. Deb unfolds it and reads it carefully. Both sides, twice. Maybe it will take her the entire fifty minutes.

She finally looks up at me. "I think this is a wonderful platform from which to begin our therapeutic program."

"Begin?" I say with disbelief. "What have all these months past been?"

"Prologue," she says.

"You're changing the game—I mean—*my plan* again." This isn't fair. She keeps asking me for more.

"I'll make you a deal, Taylor." She holds up the list. "If we can address and explore all these fears—"

"You never said that was part of this. When I wrote the list, I didn't know it was going to turn into an *exercise.*"

She waits for me to finish. "If you remain open and honest with me throughout the process, then you will have completed your rehabilitative program."

"How long will that take?"

"That's entirely up to you."

If it were entirely up to me, my program would be finished today. Right now. I want real figures—two weeks? Two months? But asking her is a waste of time. She never gives me the answers I want.

"What do you mean by open and honest?"

"That means no lying, no hiding, no making up stories. From this point on, we work as a team."

A team. If I make this deal, there's no way I'll be able to lie or tell her what I think she wants to hear. I'm going to have to tell her the truth and talk about things that are private and painful.

But if I don't make the deal, that just means more time in Sunny Meadows.

"Fine," I say.

"One more thing," she says. "At the end of your program, you're going to have to choose who you're going to live with primarily. Your mother or your father. I want you to be thinking about that decision between now and then."

I thought they would decide for me. For the first time, I'm torn about it. My mom is the obvious choice because she lets me do whatever I want and, for the most part, we get along well. But then there was the last conversation I had with my dad, where things seemed to be getting better between us. But it was only five minutes. What about five hours? Five days? Five months? If things don't work out between us, he might send me back to Sunny Meadows, or someplace worse.

That afternoon I go down to the garden for the first time in more than a week. A.J. has filled his beds with compost, and they look ripe and ready for planting. Mine look dead and abandoned.

"I guess you won the bet," I say to him when he gets there.

"We never shook on it. And you don't have to worry about that evaluation. I only have good things to say."

I look up at him. I don't understand how he can still be so nice to me after all I've put him through. "How are you doing this?" I ask. "How can you even stand to look at me?"

"You were never hard to look at. It's more when you open your mouth."

"Seriously, A.J."

He shakes his head. "I don't know. I guess I just . . . get you. Even when you're being a pain, I know why you're doing it. Of course, if you want to start being nice . . ."

I do want to be nice to him, and not because of some peer review. "What should we do now?" I ask, looking at our two mismatched plots.

"Well, we could try working together."

I hesitate for a moment, unsure, but I want to try. "Okay, let's do it."

We spend the rest of the afternoon readying my beds for planting, pulling compost from both our piles. We discuss which plants to try out. We argue a little and finally decide on Bibb lettuce, red cabbage, collard greens, chives, and carrots.

He says we can do peas and tomatoes on the next round, when the weather is a little warmer.

We put it to Dr. Deb that same day and by our next garden day, we've got the seeds and we're ready to plant.

"How long will it take them to sprout?" I ask him after we've planted all six rows.

"Depends." He looks up at the sky, and I follow his gaze. Blazing blue and not a cloud in sight. "You want to wait for rain or water them in today?"

I'm a little impatient to see them sprout. We've spent a whole lot of time on preparation; I want to see some results. Not just for my rehabilitative team, but for us.

"Let's water them in today."

He hands me the hose, and I stand over the rich black soil, letting the mist fall over the ground like sweet morning rain.

"Careful not to let the water puddle up," he says. "It'll float the seeds."

I move the spray along, letting the water soak in before I return to the same spot. "How do you know all this about gardening?"

"My mom keeps a garden. Always has."

I wonder if he remembers when I told him about my grandmother's garden. I think back to our time in the basement and how different we were then. Me, so wild and desperate to leave, and him, silent and distrustful.

I glance up to see him staring at me with a thoughtful expression, so I turn the hose on him, soaking his shirtfront, and he hops away like a frog, laughing.

Later, as we're putting our tools back in the shed, he stops and looks at me as he hasn't in a long time, searching my eyes in the gloom of the shed, without anger or distrust.

"I've missed you," he says.

I've missed you. To miss someone, you have to really know them, and I believe, despite our differences, he did know me. The real me. I study the dirt caked under my fingernails because I have no clue how to respond. I wonder if he knows I'm a different person now. Better or worse, I haven't yet decided.

"I've missed you, too," I say at last, then think up a reason to get out of there quick, before my feelings get any more muddy and confusing.

"Fear Number Four," Dr. Deb says to me the next week, reading from my list. "Turning into my mother."

We're sitting at our bench by the garden, our new therapy spot. We've gotten through *Fear Number 2: The feeling* and *Fear Number 3: Losing my mind*, which kind of go together. Then we skipped over this one and tackled other fears, which seemed easy in comparison. Because this one is a real possibility. And my mother is a subject that gets the feeling going in my chest. But I have my breathing. I count down the seconds it takes to exhale. Everything has a measure. One breath at a time.

"It's been a couple weeks since I talked to her," I tell Dr. Deb. I think about the last time, when my mother told me she met this guy, Mickey or Mikey, I can't remember. Mickey has a motorcycle and offered to take my mom out West with him on a road trip. She's always wanted to see the Grand Canyon. They left sometime last week, but she never stopped by to see me.

"What does it mean to love someone, Taylor?" Dr. Deb asks me.

"I don't know." I pick at a knot of wood in the tabletop, scraping my fingernail across it. "It means you . . . take care of them."

"So then, isn't love also being taken care of?"

"I guess so."

"Who wants to take care of you?"

My fingernail scratches two *T*s in the soft wood—Taylor Truwell. "My dad does, in his own way."

"What about your mother?"

I shake my head without meaning to. "She tries, but . . . she can barely take care of herself."

"How does that make you feel?"

"I don't know." I imagine where my mother might be right

now, in a new city, with a new boyfriend and a new adventure. Does Mickey know about her troubled daughter or that she's not yet divorced? Does he know she's an alcoholic, or is she trying to be someone else—someone better—for him? My anger wells up inside me, making my throat thick. That she would be a better person for a stranger, but not for me, her own daughter.

"It makes me mad," I tell Dr. Deb.

"Why, Taylor?"

"Because she's . . . my mother. If she won't take care of me, then who will?"

I stop talking and close my eyes. Dr. Deb waits for me to work through it. I take deep breaths. *I am powerful. I am strong. I am in control.* Finally I'm ready to continue.

"Sometimes I just think that . . . maybe if I'd been better, easier . . . I don't know."

"It's not your fault, Taylor," Dr. Deb says. "Your mother's alcoholism is not your fault. Her choices are her own."

I study my initials scratched on the wood. I know in my head Dr. Deb's right, but in my heart I have doubts. In the silence that follows I recall a time when I was a little girl, four or five years old, and my mother and I were at the playground by our old house, and I was swinging up so high that my feet kissed the sky. *Higher!* I'd scream, and she'd push me, laughing. There were no shadows on her face, no ghosts in her eyes, and even now, the memory of that moment is so clear in my mind. Because the times when she seemed truly happy were precious and so few.

"I'd like to do a role-playing exercise with you," Dr. Deb says. "But it's going to take some courage on your part. Do you trust me?"

I nod. I think I trust her. I do.

"Pretend I'm your mother," she says. "I'm sitting here across from you. You can ask me any question. You can tell me anything and I will listen."

"Okay." I try to clear my head and breathe deep. I stare into Dr. Deb's warm gaze and imagine it's my mother sitting across from me. She's sober and listening. What do I say?

"Why do you drink?" I say.

"I drink to escape my reality."

"What's wrong with your . . . reality?"

"I don't know. I only know that I'm unhappy."

"Is it . . . because of me?" I ask, fearing the answer.

"No, not because of you. You're the best thing to ever happen to me."

I'm quiet for a long moment. I don't believe her.

"If I'm the best thing to ever happen to you, then why can't you just . . . fix yourself?"

"I don't know how to fix myself."

It's true. My mother doesn't know how to fix herself. She's

tried rehab and going to AA meetings, but nothing's worked for her. Maybe she doesn't know what's wrong or she doesn't want to change. Maybe she's just given up.

"I'm mad at you," I say.

"Why are you mad at me, Taylor?"

"You're a bad mother," I say. Tears gum up my eyes. "You broke your promise to me. You left me again and again. I needed a mother. I need you now and you're not here. You say you love me, but you don't."

"I love you, Taylor. But I'm not a responsible parent."

I stand up and pace back and forth next to the picnic table. I'm so angry at her, for lying to me and leaving me. For not loving her life—and me—enough to make it work.

"I don't want to hate you," I say.

"You don't have to hate me."

"I want you to get better."

"You can't change me."

I sit down and bury my head in my arms. Love isn't enough. Hate means even less. Anger is destruction. I can't change my mother, and I can't fix her. I feel more powerless than ever before.

Dr. Deb sits beside me. She rubs my shoulders and smooths back my hair. If only my mother would stop drinking, we could be together, happy.

"You're strong, Taylor. Aren't you?"

"Yes," I say. I don't feel strong at all.

"What are you?"

I take a moment to steady my voice. Whether or not I believe it, I say the words, "I'm strong, I'm powerful, and I'm in control."

Dr. Deb squeezes me tight. "Yes, you are."

CHAPTER 20

Every other afternoon I go down to the garden to water in the seeds. The white noise of the spray and the Zen of watching the mist fall on the dirt has a tranquilizing effect on me. I hum the melodies of my grandmother's songs and remember a few more words each time. A.J.'s always nearby, turning over compost or edging off the grass so it doesn't encroach on our beds. I offer to give him a turn with the hose, but he says I'm the hydration specialist and that he prefers my singing to his own.

After a week goes by and still nothing's sprouted, I begin to have doubts.

"Maybe I'm watering them too much," I say to him. He stands beside me, pitchfork in hand, chewing on a stalk of grass and wearing a straw hat I make fun of but secretly find pretty adorable.

"You're doing fine."

"What if they're duds?"

"All of them? Duds?"

"Maybe they were microwaved." I read somewhere that microwaving seeds kills them.

He chuckles. "Who would do that?"

"Maybe it was an accident. Someone thought they were tiny bags of popcorn and, oops."

He nudges my shoulder and smiles disarmingly, which gets the soda bubbles going in my stomach. "Maybe they're not ready yet. Have a little faith."

The next day we see the first shoots poking through the soil, delicate green limbs with heavy leaf heads, lifting their faces to the sun. A small miracle. A.J. kneels beside me in the dirt. I think this must be the right time.

"There's some things I've been meaning to say to you," I tell him, pinching a clump of dirt between my fingers and watching it burst in my hand.

"What's that?"

"That I'm . . ." I pause and take a deep breath. "I'm sorry. For shutting you out all those months. I'm sorry for a lot of things."

"Me too. I was being selfish, trying to keep you here."

"You were just trying to protect me."

"I didn't do a very good job of it."

I nod slowly. We were both wrong, because we both lied and deceived each other and ratted each other out. I remember that night of the bonfire when I screamed at him like I was possessed and then the residual anger I couldn't seem to shake. Looking back now, it seems like such a waste of time and energy.

"Listen," he says after a minute, "there's something I want you to know too." But instead of finishing, he picks up a handful of dirt and rakes through it with his fingers like he's searching for worms.

"What is it?" I'm starting to get worried.

He shakes his head. "I don't want to scare you."

What could he possibly say that would scare me? "You won't."

He smiles again, bashfully this time, like he's embarrassed.

"It's just that . . . I like . . . being with you," he says.

"Being with me? Here, in the garden?"

"Here, there, wherever. I just . . . like you." He searches my eyes. "But you know that, right?"

I stare at my hands, at the dirt caked into the crevices of my palms, tiny rivers of earth. I remember our one almost kiss in the basement and the feeling I get whenever I see him here in the garden. But I can't admit those feelings to him. It's too soon. I'm still figuring out how to be his friend.

"Is that okay?" he asks.

I am powerful. I am strong. I am in control.

I am . . . scared?

"I don't know," I say at last. It's my most honest answer.

"That's okay." He squeezes my shoulder and stands up, then hands me the hose to water the new seedlings. "Back to work."

• • •

"I think I might like A.J.," I say to Margo on the phone that week.

"*Finally.*"

"What are you talking about?"

"I mean, it's about time. Have you kissed him yet?"

"No."

"Why not?"

"Because relationships between the sexes are to remain platonic?" It's the easiest answer.

She giggles. "Because you follow the rules, right?"

Maybe I should be offended by this, but I'm not. "I don't know. I guess I'm just . . . apprehensive." Apprehensive is a nicer word for scared.

"Of what?"

"What if he dumps me?"

"He won't."

"But what if he does?" I'm powerful, I'm strong, and I'm in control, but even I have my limits.

"Oh, Taylor, he's so into you. You should have seen him when you first came off the first floor and that crazed safety bot was guarding you. That's the first time I ever heard him talk, you know. He was talking about you."

I broke through his silence, without ever meaning to.

"I don't know, Margo, it seems like we're just now getting along again. I don't want to rush things or ruin what we've got."

"You won't, Taylor. It'll be just like now, only better. Like when you smile. It's still you, only prettier."

"What if he realizes I'm not that great after all?"

But she's no longer listening to me. Instead she's singing, "A.J. and Taylor, sitting in the tree. K-I-S-S—"

"Margo!" I shout into the phone, loud enough to hopefully rupture her eardrum.

"You can't stop it from coming, Taylor, so when it does, you'd better be ready."

"When what comes? What are you talking about?"

She sighs blissfully. "L-O-V-E. Love."

I try to dismiss Margo's prediction, but over the next few weeks I can't help but examine A.J. a little more closely. Not at school, where everyone is watching and the safeties are always at our backs, but in the afternoons when it's just the two of us, in our little green oasis with the dirt below and the sky above, and there seem to be so many possibilities for normal. . . .

We trim lettuce leaves and drop them in a basket for the kitchen to use in a salad. I can't stop staring at his bare shoulders or the way his muscles move under his skin as he reaches for a leaf, the rusty blond hairs on his arms that glint with sweat in the sunlight. I can't help imagining how it would feel to draw my hands along the muscles in his back and touch his skin. To have him touch me . . .

The spring air is seriously messing with my head.

We rinse the lettuce and snack on the stragglers. They're juicy and sweet, and when I stop chewing, I find him staring at me with a curious expression.

"What is it?" I say, thinking I must have lettuce stuck in my teeth.

"You're so . . . damn . . . pretty."

I swallow hard and fight the heat that's rising in my throat. Why does he have to say things like that, without any warning and completely out of nowhere? It only complicates an already complicated situation.

"And when you do that," he says.

"When I do what?"

"Get embarrassed."

I duck my head and try to act normal. "Who says I'm embarrassed?"

He shakes his head. "Your face is saying it right now." He keeps staring at me, which makes me blush even more, and just when I think it can't possibly get any worse he says, "I was just wondering what it might be like to kiss you."

I focus on the ground. I absolutely cannot look at him because I have no idea what my face is saying. I don't know how I feel or what I want.

"I've thought about it way too much," he says. "Sometimes I wonder if we were on the outside and I was just some guy you knew . . . Would you let me kiss you?"

I exhale slowly and decide to be completely honest with him. Even if it's embarrassing—my inexperience—it's the truth.

"I've known a lot of guys on the outside," I say. "And I never let them kiss me."

"Really?" He seems surprised.

"Really."

He takes a step toward me, closing the gap between us. My heart quickens and my olfactory is on overdrive. I love the way he smells, even when he's sweaty and dirty, maybe even more then. I watch as a bead of sweat traces a line down his throat, then follow that trail up to his jaw and the scar on his lip. The story of that scar is one I still don't know, but I want to. I like him—a lot. But I'm so afraid to ruin this great thing we have going. What if things get weird between us? What if I do something to drive him away? What if, what if, what if?

"What's wrong?" he says. His eyebrows dip with concern. I can barely make any sense in my head, much less out loud, when he's staring at me like that. I back away from him slowly.

"I just . . . I don't want to lose your friendship."

"You won't," he says, and I know at this moment, he means it. But feelings are conditional. They change with the wind.

"What you're feeling, A.J., that lasts for as long as it's easy. When things get hard, people leave. People you love leave you."

He shakes his head slowly. "I'm not people, Taylor, and this isn't easy. Pretending I don't like you. Especially when I know you must feel—"

"I'm not a fun girl, A.J. I'm difficult and stubborn and sometimes I'm just . . . mean."

"Yeah, I know."

I scowl at him. "You're not perfect either."

"I never said I was."

I squat down and bite at my thumbnail, which is gritty and tastes like dirt, but I don't care. Already things are changing. Feelings breed more feelings, uncertainty and insecurity, and soon enough our nice, steady stream becomes turbulent and unpredictable. I know he's standing there waiting for an answer, but I don't want to have to choose. All or nothing is too great a risk.

"Look," he says finally, after my silence can only mean one thing. "I'm not going to pressure you. You want to be friends. Fine, we're friends. I won't bother you about it anymore."

He gathers up our tools while I continue to stare at the ground and mentally add another fear to the list.

Fear Number 38: Losing A.J.

The next day I invite McKenzie and Charlotte down to the garden to show them how our plants are really taking off. It's looking like a real garden now and not just a few rows of dirt.

But there's another reason. It's too dangerous with just A.J. and me—too much awkwardness, too much time alone.

The three of us girls walk down the hill together after school. McKenzie brings her sketch pad, finds a sunny place to sit, and draws—beautiful, true-to-life pictures of the plants and bugs, capturing details down to the wrinkles in the cabbage leaves and the veined pattern of a dragonfly's wing.

A.J. lets Charlotte use a pair of his gardening gloves, and together they transplant baby tomato plants we've grown from seed. At first she's nervous about it, but A.J. has a way of explaining things, of making people feel confident in what they're doing. Soon enough she relaxes. He told me once that he'd like to be a teacher someday. I think he'd be great at it.

Over the next few weeks they come back again and again. McKenzie isn't too interested in the gardening aspect of it, preferring to draw or nap in the sun, but Charlotte has a real interest and suggests we put in a butterfly garden. McKenzie draws the design for it, and we all research what flowers to put in to attract butterflies. Dr. Deb brings us plants from the nursery, and Charlotte directs the planting. It's pretty awesome seeing her take ownership of the garden, and when the first butterfly comes to visit, Charlotte reaches out and hugs me for the first time.

But there are days when McKenzie and Charlotte can't come because of therapy or group, and then it's just A.J. and me, and all the things I cannot say.

We pull weeds side by side and I feel the distance between us, space that I asked for and received. I hate it—this invisible barrier that I constructed. Just like that game Dr. Deb and I used to play, Yes or No. I told him no, and now he is farther from me than before.

We pick a batch of ripe carrots and wash them off in the hose, then sit together in the grass, nibbling like rabbits. Without thinking I reach over to wipe a smudge of dirt off his upper lip, and my thumb grazes his scar. In that moment when my skin touches his, I realize what a terrible mistake I've made. That I had the chance to be with someone wonderful and special and *real*, who thinks I'm worth caring for, who likes me in spite of my flaws.

He stops chewing and stares at me quizzically. I lean in closer, thinking to skip the trouble of words and just kiss him, when he suddenly starts choking.

"Carrot," he gasps between coughs. I smack his back a few times, and he leans forward and spits out the orange bits. I grab the hose and offer him a trickle of water. He clears his throat and he's fine. But now I'm thinking about the moment before he choked, and from the look on his face, he is too.

"Were you . . . ," he says. "Was that, um . . . ?"

I sit on the ground and stare at my hands. I can't believe how not smooth I am. He scoots closer and touches his finger to my chin, tilting my face upward.

"I'm sorry," I say. "I just—"

"Shh. Just nod your head if I can kiss you."

I nod slowly. A second later his mouth covers mine, and I taste the carrots and hose water on his tongue, sweet and a little metallic. He stops to look at me, as if checking to see if this is okay.

I nod again.

He pulls me to him. This time I wrap my arms around his neck and kiss back because I want to show him how much he means to me, after all this time. His hand slides up my back and rests on the nape of my neck, gently squeezing. My skin tingles, and I shiver from the sensation.

We break away when the safety makes his rounds. A.J. pretends to be digging in the dirt while I pick up the hose, even though the plants are plenty watered. As soon as the safety moves along, he grabs for me, but I slip away and aim the nozzle at his heart. He lifts both hands in the air.

"You win," he says with a smile.

"No matter what happens," I say, "you have to be my friend."

"I will *always* be your friend."

I lower the hose a little. "Do you think this is the right thing to do?"

He tilts his head and says with a mischievous smile, "Of course I do."

I pull the trigger to wipe that smug smile off his face, but his reflexes are too fast. He dodges and grabs for the hose, easily maneuvering it away from me and aiming it over my head, drenching me in a cold shower. I yelp and tackle him to the ground, where we wrestle for control of the hose. We're both muddy and laughing and somewhere in the struggle the hose ends up out of our reach, spraying water up into the air, shrouding us in a fine mist of rain. He leans over me, his face just inches from mine, his eyelashes wet, his face beaded with water, and his gray eyes so beautiful and true.

I close my eyes as his lips brush against mine.

There is no going back now.

CHAPTER 21

"I have good news."

Dr. Deb and I are sitting at our picnic bench outside. It's May now, and when the warm breeze blows, I can smell the herb plants we put in earlier that week—mint, rosemary, basil, and sage. The air is heady with their aroma. That was McKenzie's idea. She said she was tired of smelling compost, so we planted an herb garden and in the middle, we built a little wooden bench for her to sit and draw. Next we're going to build an arbor with climbing vines, to offer a little shade in the coming summer months.

"What is it?" I ask.

"Your rehabilitative team met yesterday. We've determined that you're nearing the end of your program."

I sit up straighter and look at her. Another curveball.

"The end of my program? But we're only halfway through my list."

Dr. Deb nods. "You've already tackled the biggies. Consider the rest to be . . . extra credit."

"I know, but . . ." I think about Charlotte, who's become

a really close friend. And McKenzie—who will tutor her in math? And Dr. Deb. How will I make it on the outside without her help?

And A.J. . . . we're just getting started.

"You look upset."

"I'm not upset," I say, struggling to maintain my composure. "Just . . . surprised."

"You knew this day would come, though."

I glance up at her. Of course I knew this day would come, but not so soon, not now, when life was just starting to go right for once. What about the garden? What about my mental health?

"Take a few days to digest this," she says. "We'll touch base again next week."

For the rest of the day I can't think about anything else: the possibility that in a few weeks, I might have to say goodbye to the people I know and love and trust. To A.J.

The next day in the garden A.J. and I are alone. We've constructed a trellis out of bamboo sticks for the cucumber plants to climb up, and as I place a thin green vine on the bottom rung, I realize with sudden sadness that I might not be here to see the cucumbers flower and fruit.

I stop and look around at our garden—at the tomato plants beginning to bear little green balls, the flowering squashes, the hot peppers that we're planning to make pepper jelly with. I think about everything we still have to plant—sweet peas, eggplant, another variety of tomato that's striped yellow and orange. We argued about that. A.J. wanted beefsteaks and I wanted the tiger stripes, and he said he'd let me have my way if we could pickle the cucumbers when they're ripe. But now he'll have to do it without me.

I watch A.J. setting the vines with careful, tender precision, like an artist. He glances up and catches my eye, starts to smile, then stops.

"What's wrong?"

I shake my head. "What are we doing?"

"We're training the vines," he says, then stands up straighter. "Aren't we?"

"What happens when we don't have this anymore?" I motion to the plants around us. He lays down the vine and comes to my side of the cucumber frame.

"Do you mean the garden?"

"Yes," I say, even though it's more than that. It's the space we've created, where we go to get away from everyone else and just be . . . together. It's every inside joke we share and every kindness that passes between us. It's our little arguments and make-ups. It's my calm and it's our . . . home.

"Dr. Deb said garden therapy is going well," he says carefully. "She wants to expand the program." He has no idea what's going on with me, and I'm suddenly angry at Dr. Deb for forcing me into this garden therapy and encouraging me to be open with my feelings. Why? Just so she could take it all away?

"Come here," he says, and pulls me to him. He tilts my chin to study my face, and I remember the time we were dancing and he lifted my chin, all the times he's had to lift my chin, because I'm always looking down and never up.

"What's this about?" he says.

I open my mouth to tell him what Dr. Deb said, how I'm nearing the end of my program, but there in his arms, I don't want to think about it.

"Nothing," I say. "I had a moment. But it's over."

I reach my arms around his neck and pull his face toward mine, kissing him long and deeply, trying to erase the worry lines on his face and my own desperate thoughts.

I'm not leaving. Not yet. Somehow I'll make Dr. Deb understand.

"I had the feeling last night."

It's my next therapy session, and I've resolved to buy more time. I'm not fully rehabilitated yet. I just need to show that to Dr. Deb.

"Really?" Dr. Deb says. "It's been a while. What do you think triggered it?"

"I don't know. Maybe it's my anxiety over my mom. Because I haven't talked to her in so long."

"Maybe," she says. She's nodding her head in agreement, but she doesn't seem too concerned about it.

"I don't think the breathing is enough anymore. Maybe you should teach me another exercise. Just in case."

Dr. Deb seems to consider this. "Perhaps your anxiety is a result of you nearing the end of your program. Maybe, you're . . . apprehensive about leaving?"

"Why would I be apprehensive?"

"Well, it's another unknown for you. And you have friends here. Dear friends. And you know that I'm here to listen and help you process your emotions. Maybe you don't think you're strong enough yet."

"Well, if you think I need more time . . ."

She smiles. "You're ready, Taylor. Pushing back your release date won't make it any easier. But of course we can talk about any feelings you might be having between now and then."

I run my fingers over the grooved wood of the tabletop. She's seen through me, predicted it even. Dr. Deb always seems to know what I'm going to do or say before I do.

"No, I'm fine," I say. "If you don't mind, I think I'd like to process these emotions on my own."

She nods and leaves me at the picnic bench, where I stare at the garden and sow the seeds of a new plan. Even if Dr.

Deb thinks I'm ready, she's just one member of my rehabilitative team, and there are others who might disagree.

There's no time to waste, so the next morning I put my plan
in action. I start by stashing a pair of sharps into my backpack
in first period. Sulli and Brandi watch me do it, and both
stare at me like I've lost my marbles.

"You can tell on me," I say, which is a mistake, because
it only confuses them more. Class seems to take forever to
get through. Finally Mr. Chris collects the sharps and counts
them up. But he must not remember how many he began
with, because he doesn't realize one pair is gone.

"I think there's one missing," I offer, one step away from
waving the scissors in front of his face.

Mr. Chris shakes his head. "Nope. All here."

I roll my eyes and drop them into the box on my way out.
My next opportunity for rule breaking doesn't come until
after lunch in the pen, where I ask McKenzie for a cigarette.

"Not here," she says, glancing both ways to where safeties
are standing on either side of us.

"It's fine. I won't tell them you gave it to me."

"You don't even smoke."

"It's part of therapy," I say, completely lying. "It's a new
method Dr. Deb and I are trying out."

She shrugs and pulls one out of her bra. It's slightly damp and smells like perfume, but I stick it in my mouth like I know what I'm doing. I've watched my mother, Margo, and McKenzie smoke cigarettes a million times. How hard can it be?

McKenzie's fishing in her bra for her matches when A.J. walks out of the lunchroom. It's too late to hide it. He sees me and immediately makes his way over.

"What are you doing?" he says to me.

"Trying new things." I strike up the match and hold it to the end of the cigarette, but nothing really happens. Then I remember I have to suck while lighting, so I purse my lips and take a tremendous breath. Smoke fills my lungs instantaneously; tears run down my cheeks, my throat is on fire, and I can't stop coughing. My lungs feel like they're being rubbed against a cheese grater. How can people stand it?

McKenzie retrieves the cigarette and takes a few quick puffs before putting it out under her boot—she's a frugal girl—while A.J. smacks my back harder than necessary.

Finally the smoke clears and I'm able to stand straight again.

"How'd you like it?" he asks me.

"Not much."

For the rest of the day, I plot. I need to skip the small stuff and do something explosive, something that will send me right to the first floor. That always gets their attention. It seemed so easy before, when I wasn't faking it. I wish Margo were here—she was the expert at this sort of thing. If this is going to convince anyone, it has to be an inside job, which means I need help.

"You want me to do what?" McKenzie says to me later that day after I've outlined my plan to her.

"Just act like you're really scared of me. Maybe we got into a fight or something. Maybe I think you're messing around with A.J."

"Eww, gross. That'd be like kissing my dad."

I shake my head. "Focus, McKenzie. Just use it for motivation. You have to make it look real. Can you fake cry?"

She tilts her head, and her lower lip droops a little. After a few more seconds, her eyes get watery and sad.

"Great," I say. "You ready?"

She sniffles a little and nods her head. "Wait, why are you doing this again?"

"Because they're trying to release me and I'm not ready to go yet."

She looks at me strangely. "You really are crazy."

I mess up her hair a little bit and then grab my comb dagger. I tell her to take a couple of laps around the room so it looks like she's under duress. "Enough," I say when she's breathing heavy, which doesn't take very long, maybe because she's a smoker. "Let's go."

She runs screaming down the hall. The screaming is a nice touch and really sets the tone. The girls all rush to their doorways, which is crucial, Margo would say, since the audience is a necessary component of performance art. I stalk down the hallway after her, holding the comb high in the air like I'm going to stab her with it.

"She's insane!" McKenzie screams. Rhonda comes out of her office and blocks my path. I decide to do something drastic—I push her off me and continue on down the hall. Her massive hand grabs the back of my shirt and drops me on my butt on the hallway floor. Ouch. I'd forgotten how painful resistance can be.

"Taylor, what's going on?" Tabitha asks as McKenzie hides behind her, using her as a human shield. Tabitha shakes her head and holds up her hands like I must have some rational explanation for all this. I muster up my crazy face.

"I want to see your blood," I snarl at McKenzie, and make a few jabbing motions with the comb to really bring it home.

Tabitha looks helplessly to Rhonda, who hauls me to my feet. The nice thing about safeties is they're not swayed by motives. They see misbehavior, they take you down and ask questions later. "Let's go," Rhonda says.

"This isn't over!" I shout over my shoulder at McKenzie. Only I can see her strange little smile.

•   •   •

"Can you please explain to me what happened yesterday on the second floor?"

We're sitting at the therapy bench, and I've decided to take this thing all the way. If I can convince Dr. Deb that I'm mad with jealousy, then maybe she'll allow me enough time to work through it. Even though it's off-limits, she knows about A.J. and my relationship, supports it even, as a way for me to "express my feelings."

"McKenzie and A.J. are messing around," I say to her. It's a total lie, but imagining it gets me angry enough to fake it.

"Are you sure of that?" Dr. Deb asks.

"I saw them kissing in the garden."

She sits back and considers this piece of information, which can't possibly be denied, if I saw it myself.

"That doesn't sound like A.J."

She's right. It doesn't sound like him. But I have to make her believe it, if I want us to be together.

"He's just another guy, right?"

"Have you confronted him about it?"

"No."

"I think you should."

"Whatever. It's just more of the same. As soon as you let people in, they stomp all over you." I slouch forward and cross my arms while Dr. Deb studies me. I know if I sit there much longer, I'll confess everything.

"Would you mind if we cut it short today?" I ask.

"No, I don't mind," she says.

Then I decide to drop one last line, one that I know will affect her. A little bit of reverse psychology.

"I really can't wait to get out of here," I say, and walk off before she has time to reply.

The next afternoon I head down to the garden, even though it might look suspicious, if A.J.'s supposed to be cheating on me and I still choose to be around him. But maybe not too suspicious, since daytime talk shows abound with cheaters and the women who forgive them.

When I get there, he's pulling weeds while McKenzie sketches nearby. Seeing them together like that, so innocently going about their own business, makes me feel guilty about the lies I've told. But I did it for a reason. I did it for us.

A.J. stands tall, drops his pile of weeds to the ground, and looks at me with simmering anger. I've got a very bad feeling about this as I look to McKenzie for a sign.

"He didn't hear it from me," she says, standing and snapping shut her sketchbook. "Besides, this is your crazy town. I'm just visiting."

She leaves to walk up the hill, and I glance back at A.J. His face appears to be made of rock, his lips pressed so tightly together, they've lost their color. I know why—he's so angry he can't speak.

"How's it going?" I say, trying to keep it light.

"Guess who brought me into their office after school today?"

"I don't know," I say cautiously. "Who?"

"Dr. Deb."

Oh, crap.

"She told me your little story," he continues. "About how you caught McKenzie and me kissing in the garden."

Crap, crap, crap.

"Why would you say that?" he asks with pain in his eyes. "Are you trying to break up with me or something?"

"No," I say. "It's not that at all."

"I don't understand you." He rakes his hand through his hair, getting crumbs of dirt all in it. "Stealing sharps, smoking cigarettes, lying to your therapist." He stops and looks at me as the realization dawns on his face. "You're getting released, aren't you?"

"How'd you know about the sharps?"

"Sulli told me. He said you *told him* to tell on you."

"Oh." I lock my knees because I suddenly feel like I might collapse. I feel so stupid and childish. I shouldn't have lied, but I did it for a good reason. Can't he see that?

"So that's it, then?"

I nod and stare at the ground. I can't look at him.

"Why didn't you tell me?"

"I wanted to, but . . . I thought maybe I could get it changed."

"What? By lying?"

I glare up at him, mad that he's judging me, when all I'm trying to do is keep us together.

"Yes, A.J. By lying. Because I'm a *liar*."

"I never said that."

"But that's what you're thinking. First I lie to leave. Then I lie to stay. Everything I say is a lie."

I feel the tears coming, and I don't want to cry in front of him and confirm just how weak and crazy I am. I turn to walk away, and he grabs my arm.

"Stop," he says. "Stay here and let's talk about this."

But I don't want to talk. I'm sick and tired of talking—about feelings and what I want, what I'm afraid of. It doesn't make a bit of difference, because here I am again, lost and alone. About to be kicked out and abandoned, again.

"No touching," a safety barks, and we both look up. But it's not the safety who surprises me.

It's my mother.

CHAPTER 22

A.J. immediately lets go and takes a step back. My mother takes stock of the situation, removes her sunglasses, and stares him down. But more than the warning look in her eyes, they are rid of the poison. Her eyes are lucid and clear as the bright, blue sky.

"Mom," I say slowly. She holds out her arms, and without thinking, I go to her. She hugs me tightly, strongly. All I smell on her neck is perfume.

"Baby, I've missed you so much."

I remember we're not alone and glance back to see A.J. standing there, looking a little lost and forlorn.

"Mom, this is A.J., my . . ." I falter a little and see the safety still standing nearby. "My friend."

A flicker of pain crosses A.J.'s eyes, but he quickly recovers.

"We've met before," she says with a tight smile. I remember when she came with my dad and I had the panic attack on the lawn. They must have met then.

A.J. nods, glancing between us.

"Come see the garden," I say to escape the weird tension

between them. I walk her up and down the rows, pointing out all that's above- and belowground, our compost piles, the worm bin, our herb and butterfly gardens, which also attract the occasional hummingbird. I pick a sprig of rosemary and hand it to her. She puts it to her nose and inhales deeply. "This is wonderful," she says. I glance over to see A.J. half-hidden behind the tomatoes—weeding—but I know he's listening.

"I'd really like for us to catch up," she says. "Is there someplace private we can talk?"

"Yeah. Sure."

I lead her over to the picnic bench and sit down across from her. I remember role-playing with Dr. Deb. Could I say those things to my mother here and now, while she's sober? Do I want to?

"This seems like a nice enough place," she says.

"It's grown on me," I say, recalling the expression A.J. used a long time ago. There's really no other way to describe it. It happened without me knowing it.

"Your father says you'll be getting out soon."

"That's what they tell me."

"I'm coming home too," she says.

"What happened to Mickey?"

"Oh, you know . . ." She waves her hand dismissively. "He liked to party too much, and I'm . . . past that now."

I narrow my eyes at her. Since when is my mother past "partying," which is a loose translation for drinking? I think of how absent she's been from my life since I came to Sunny Meadows. All the times I called her cell phone and got no response, the weeks that went by without word from her.

"So, why the visit?" I ask. "Now, after all this time?"

"Because I wanted to see you. I love you, Taylor, and . . . I want you to come home. I've put down a deposit on a nice apartment for us, and I've got some job interviews lined up. I'd like us to give it another try."

"What about your drinking?"

"I'm done with it," she says. "I'm done forever."

I cross my arms and study her. She looks sober, acts sober, but I've been through this before. She's sober for as long as it's easy.

"Baby, I know what my illness has done to you. I know that it's my fault you're here. And I want to make it right."

I study the tabletop, which I've memorized by now, every groove and knot of wood, every splinter. I want to believe her, I want it so badly, but she's lied to me so many times before.

"I don't expect an answer right now," she says. "I'm just asking you to think about it."

I want to give her another chance. Maybe we really could make it work. Then I see her open purse on the table, a small bottle of Perrier peeking out. The seal is broken, but the bottle is completely full. I have a flashback to when I was twelve years old at my dance recital, coming out of the dressing room to find my mom so drunk she could barely stand. My dad had already left, so one of the other parents had to drive us home. I quit dance after that, I was so embarrassed. At the time I had no idea how she'd gone from completely sober to completely wasted in the course of two hours. Until days later when I found the Perrier bottle in the recycling bin, stinking like vodka.

I study the bottle in her purse, so tempted to pull it out and see for myself. But I don't, because I don't want to have to go around checking bottles to see if she's been drinking, or wait up for her at night worrying when she'll come home. I don't want to watch her mess around with men she doesn't love or see her wear a mask for the world. I don't want to have to always try and make things pleasant so she doesn't have a reason to go drinking. I don't want to do any of it anymore.

But she needs me.

I see my initials carved into the table—TT. I've done so much work here at this table, and in the garden, in the classroom. My mom loves me, but she can't take care of me. I have to take care of myself.

"Look, Mom," I say to her. "When I get out, I'm going to live with Dad. I think that's the best thing for me for now."

She stares at me blankly, trying to use the mask on me, but I know her too well. I'm hurting her feelings, but these are the words that need to be said.

"I want you to be sober," I continue. "I want you to *stay* sober, but you have to do it for yourself, not for me."

She nods slowly and glances over at the dorms. "Seems like this place has done its job."

I don't know what she means by it, and I don't feel like asking. Maybe therapy never worked for her because she never really wanted to change. And I have changed. I'm not just *her daughter* anymore, a reflection of her happy and sad times, trying to keep it together for the both of us. I'm my own person. And from here on out, I'm making decisions for myself.

"I'm sorry, Mom."

She nods but won't look at me. She's ashamed, looking downward and never up. "I just want you to know," she begins, "that I love you, and you always have a home with me. No matter what." She glances around, looking lost. "It's getting late. I should be going."

She stands, and I hope she's not leaving to go get a drink. The thought of it makes me sick, but I can't control her. I can't make her want to change.

"I love you, Mom," I say, and hug her tightly.

"Good-bye, baby."

"Good-bye."

She makes her way back toward the dorms, and I watch her retreating form until she disappears over the crest of the hill. I turn to see A.J. a few yards away, watching me.

I am not my mother.

I head back to the garden, where his arms are already open to me. "I should have told you," I say, burying my face in his chest. "About being released. I shouldn't have lied."

"I know why you did it." He runs his fingers delicately over my face, and I peer into his gray eyes, full of forgiveness and understanding.

"I'm leaving," I say to him.

He nods. He's already accepted it.

"I love you," I say, because I know it's true and there's no good reason not to tell him.

He smiles and squeezes me tighter. "I love you, too."

He kisses me, and I want to hold on to this moment forever because soon I'll be leaving Sunny Meadows and I must face the fact that I might never see him again. Our future is scary and uncertain, but right now, we're here together and we love each other.

This is real. This is the truth.

CHAPTER 23

Dr. Deb sets up a video call with my dad the next week. It's the last thing that needs to be done in order to complete all my rehabilitative goals. I've begun imagining what it will be like to be out in the world again. Equal parts scary and exciting.

"As you know, Mr. Truwell," Dr. Deb says to her computer monitor, where my dad's face lights up the screen, "I've asked you to join us today so that you and Taylor can discuss your future living situation, specifically with regards to boundaries."

She turns the screen toward me, and my dad and I stare at each other, waiting for the other one to speak.

"I dusted your room," he says, "and washed the sheets. I figured you might want to pick out a new comforter."

"Great. Thanks for . . . sprucing it up."

"You'll have to help me with the grocery list. I don't know what you like to eat anymore."

"I'm not too picky." After eight months here, the one thing I've never gotten used to is the food.

"I guess we'll need some rules then," he says. "First off, no going out on school nights. And on the weekends, a curfew. How about ten p.m.? We can work up from there."

I smile, because I remember how we used to fight about this before. Back when I was accustomed to staying out all night if I felt like it. But right now, a ten o'clock curfew seems like ultimate freedom.

"Ten is good."

He smiles a little and seems surprised at my willingness to compromise.

"And you're going to have to keep your grades up. You're an A student, Taylor. You need to think about your future. Colleges care about GPA."

"You're right," I say, and I mean it. I've begun to want things again, like an education. Maybe if I do well enough my senior year, I can still get into a university. But if not, there's junior college.

"How about you?" he says. "Do you have any requests?"

I stop and think for a moment. What do I want now? "I want to keep in touch with my friends here at Sunny Meadows and with Margo. They're long-distance."

"You should probably have your own phone anyhow. I can put you on my plan, and it will be less expensive that way."

"And I want to plant a garden. Like Grandma did. Somewhere in the backyard maybe."

My father nods. "There's good light in the back. I can help you with that."

"And . . ." I stop because I don't know how to say it. "I want us to . . . talk to each other. About stuff. I want to know what's going on in your life and tell you about mine."

He smiles. "Yes, I want that too."

"Good."

"There's something else," he says. "I'm going to make you mad at some point. That's just the way it is. When that happens, just stomp around or yell at me or go for a walk, but don't . . . run away."

"I won't," I say. I'm done running.

"I know you're going to want to see your mother, and that's fine. But no overnights. You're going to be my responsibility now. For the next couple years at least."

I smile. "That sounds good, Dad. I'm ready."

"Good." He nods. "Great."

Dr. Deb takes over then, and they talk about the details of my release. I excuse myself to go down to the garden, where A.J. is waiting for me. But instead of gardening, we lie in the warm grass and stare up at the clouds, dreaming out loud. There's still so much I haven't told him and so much I still have to learn. Too soon the safety tells us it's time to go inside for dinner. I grab hold of his hand and try to keep him there with me, because it's all happening way too fast.

"This isn't the end," A.J. says, touching his thumb to my cheek and kissing me softly.

But that's exactly how it feels.

On the morning of my last day at Sunny Meadows, we have an open house in the garden. It's a way for me to say good-bye to everyone while also generating interest in garden therapy, which A.J. and Dr. Deb are planning to expand in the coming months.

People drift in and out, snacking on a cherry tomato or two, smelling the herbs, and admiring the flowers. Sulli and Brandi stop by for a visit, along with Tracy from the third floor, Rhonda, and Tabitha. Charlotte acts as the tour guide, while McKenzie displays some of her drawings on an easel and reminds people not to pick the flowers.

And of course, A.J. is there too.

Finally it's just him and me with the dirt below and the sky above and all the possibilities between us.

"I have a present for you," he says.

"Is it a key?" I tease.

"No, something much better. Hold on."

He jogs over to the maintenance shed and comes back a minute later, holding a pot in his hands. He hands it to me, and I peer at the rich black soil inside it.

"It's your favorite flower," he says.

"My favorite flower? I didn't know I had one."

"You do now."

"What is it?"

He shrugs. "You'll have to water it and see."

I stare hard at the dirt and feel my tears coming. I don't bother trying to stop them. He takes the pot and sets it on the ground, pulls me close.

"I want to see you again," I say to him.

"You will."

"How do I know for sure?"

He points to the garden, which is now teeming with life. It's hard to remember it ever being just dead grass. It seems as though it's always been there.

"Remember when we planted our first seeds?" he says, and I know what he's driving at. That week that I'd watered them and nothing sprouted. I began to think they never would, and he said to me . . .

"I have faith," I say.

"Me too."

We kiss and hold each other until a safety comes and tells me that it's time to go.

"Wait," I say to A.J., suddenly realizing there's a question I never got to ask him. "That scar on your lip—how'd you get it?"

"Fishing," he says, pulling back on an imaginary reel and letting it go. "Hooked my lip good. Didn't catch any fish that day."

"Oh," I say, panicking because there's still so much I don't know and we're suddenly out of time.

"This isn't the end," he reminds me.

I take a deep breath, and then another. This isn't the end, but I wrap my arms around his neck and kiss him like it's our last. For once, the safety doesn't interrupt us.

I leave him there in the garden. At the crest of the hill, I turn back, and he lifts one hand. But he doesn't wave, because it's *not* a good-bye. I take a mental picture to hold on to in the coming weeks and months when I'm missing him the most. If I never see him again, I know that he'll be with me still, like my grandmother. In my heart and in my head, in my bones. And I'm a better person now, a *stronger* person, having known him.

My father stands with Dr. Deb in the parking lot. He looks as nervous as I feel, but I give him a hug that is heartfelt and true. My duffel bags are already in the backseat, which means there is only one more person I need to say good-bye to.

"Thank you," I say to her, "for not giving up on me."

"Thank you," she says, "for teaching me a few new tricks."

I smile at her through my tears.

"Oh, Taylor," she says with wet eyes. "This is a happy day."

I nod, unashamed of my tears.

Dr. Deb smiles and sniffs a little. I give her a hug, and I don't ever want to let go.

But I have to.

I get into my dad's car and shut the door behind me. I cradle A.J.'s pot in my lap. My father starts up the engine, and I glance back one more time at Sunny Meadows. Dr. Deb waves, and I hear A.J.'s voice in my head reminding me, *This isn't the end.*

But here and now it is only me and my words that I now believe as truth.

I am powerful. I am strong. I am in control.

I take a deep breath and turn around just in time to see the gate open.

ACKNOWLEDGMENTS

I wish to thank:

My mom and dad for supporting, loving, and always accepting me; my sisters, lifelong friends. Jordan P and SBV. Sarah M for holding my hand. Eric N for your early encouragement with Taylor, and Andrew Kozma for the many hours you devoted to my early manuscripts.

Kathy "Kathryn" T, I love you both. Grace for accepting me into your loving-fun-crazy family. Cherie G and Sky F for your kind words and confidence. Meredith R for being there when I need you the most.

Geoff B and Tracey M for sharing your expertise. My agent, Caryn Wiseman, for your endless support and advice. My editor, Namrata Tripathi, for tumbling my rock of a story until it shone. The Atheneum team for their beautiful work with the cover, layout, and publicity.

My critique partners Heather Whitaker and Angele McQuade— brilliant writers and dear friends. I truly couldn't have done this without you both. Power of the Trinity!

My children, you are my favorites. And last, but never least, my husband—you are my beginning, middle, and end.

An unlikely romance.

A terrifying dream world.

One final chance for survival.

Nevermore

KELLY CREAGH